KILLER'S GREED

JOHN BLAZE

A Black Horse Western

ROBERT HALE · LONDON

© John Blaze 1992
First published in Great Britain 1992

ISBN 0 7090 4707 X

Robert Hale Limited
Clerkenwell House
Clerkenwell Green
London EC1R 0HT

The right of John Blaze to be identified as
author of this work has been asserted by him
in accordance with the Copyright, Designs and
Patents Act 1988.

Photoset in North Wales by
Derek Doyle & Associates, Mold, Clwyd.
Printed and bound in Great Britain by WBC Print Ltd.,
and WBC Bookbinders Ltd, Bridgend, Mid Glamorgan.

1
Murder in Greenlands

Hot and gritty sand choked his mouth. With his return to partial consciousness, his numbed mind tried to flash orders to his body. Using his arms, usually strong as ox-legs, he pushed himself up. Spitting, shaking his head, he stared at the surrounding sand.

He forced his brain to think. He realised he was not wounded – and he sure as hell wasn't dead! He could see his Stetson on the ground before him and he could feel the throbbing in his head. He touched his skull and felt the sticky blood mixed with his hair.

Sitting on his backside would not get him anywhere! He reached for his hat and put it on his head, slowly, because even that act hurt his cranium. He looked around and uttered a short, grim laugh.

He felt pretty sure he would not see Ern Spiceland. He remembered the hot angry words Ern had flung at him, the four-letter curses, and then the fight. Ern had lashed out with his fists.

Jack Griffin realised he had been punched clean off his cayuse and had probably struck his head on a rock. He did not know how long he had been out of this world but probably Ern Spiceland had rowelled his mount off the moment he had fallen.

The fight had been unexpected, taking Jack Griffin by surprise. One moment they had been exchanging caustic remarks, and then Ern's anger had spilled over, not surprising in a big-balled hombre like him!

Ten yards away his horse was still ground-hitched, nosing for green tufts of grass amid the thorn and sand.

Jack climbed back into the saddle, steadied his swimming head somehow, held the ribbons loosely and then spurred the animal on. The land around him was very arid even for this area of the Texas Panhandle. If a man wanted shade, he would have to sit under his horse's belly – and if he didn't have a horse then God help him!

He had been riding off the trails with Ern Spiceland, asking for the town of Greenlands. Early that morning Jack had ridden out of town on his hired horse and had travelled over to Ern's ranch. Then in the midday heat they had set off together for Greenlands.

Just that morning Jack had volunteered for the job of deputy sheriff of the cow town. He had offered his services when he heard that Sam Brent, the previous deputy, had been shot by an outlaw. He had taken the job on the understanding that he could quit when he figured to buy himself a ranch. Immediately Jack had been sent out to bring Ern Spiceland back to town for questioning.

'Just go git that ornery galoot,' Tom Mortimer, the rugged old sheriff of the cow town, didn't waste words. 'I'll tell you about the charge later. Spiceland has got beef on that spread of his that don't belong to him, so I'm told …'

'I like Ern – but he's a close-mouth galoot at times.'

'The hell with whether you like him or not! Just go git him an' bring him into town.'

For many miles the tree-less rolling ground belonged to the big Bar-K ranch. At the end of the plain, where the hills rose and provided a backdrop, lay Ern's poor ranch. It was a terrain where grass grew sparsely in sand and shale and rattlers basked on hot days. Ern had filed claim to the Round-O brand, and his cattle were branded thus. Ern was a bright-eyed swarthy man who said little to anyone when he came into town. Most men who knew him at all liked him.

Jack had not seen any rustled cattle on the Round-O but there was nothing conclusive about his brief inspection. The longhorns could be hidden in the foothills, in the many little blind canyons. Jack just didn't have time to look around. He had instructions to bring Ern in to Greenlands for questioning and that only. There was nothing else he had to do.

Ern had gone along, without advancing any views or objections. Sure, that had seemed a bit strange, but he had saddled his big roan and they had left together. He and Jack had met more than once in the saloons of Greenlands and had been friends. It had been 'Hi, pal! Drink?' And Jack had always agreed and then bought a beer or a rotgut whiskey for his friend.

So Jack Griffin had rowelled his hired horse and found the trail leading to town. Greenlands was a blur on the horizon – when he could see through the heat hazes. All around the territory was flat, with the endless clumps of mesquite and catclaw, hard on a horse and rider. He came across a few Bar-K cattle and the scraggy leery longhorns eyed him suspiciously. It would be roundup time in a few weeks. Maybe there was some connection between Tom Mortimer's instructions and Ern Spiceland's behaviour.

But he was returning without his man. More than that, he would be returning his deputy sheriff's badge to Tom Mortimer.

He had taken the job on only because Sam Brant lay on a bed in the back of the sheriff's office. And Sam, who had been the deputy sheriff, was severely wounded. He had been shot by Mike Capstaff. Sure the local doc had treated Sam but he was in a bad way.

Mike Capstaff was an outlaw, a cuss who rode in and out of Greenlands when he felt free. Sam Brant had found him in the Red Pine saloon but Sam had also found a gunfight and he had got the worst part of the fracas. Then, as usual after creating hell, Capstaff had ridden out of town, shaking off half-hearted pursuit.

Greenlands was a substantial roaring cow town with plenty of noisy drinking joints, cattle corrals with smelly animals and hard galoots who thought the law a joke. There were things going on in Greenlands which Jack Griffin did not like.

Jack had just returned to the county. He had spent three years as a bounty hunter, grim years which he figured were behind him. He had chased men for the sake of the price on their heads and he had got most of them, dead or alive. There were times when he had memories he could spit. He had worn two guns most of the time – and slept with them. Then he had returned to Greenlands, the town he had known as a boy.

He had been back in Greenlands just over a month. He had been staying at the Packhorse Hotel, waiting for a chance to buy a spread at a reasonable price. He had the money. It was in the bank, right there in

Greenlands, every one of the four thousand dollars he had earned hunting and killing his fellow men, even if they had been the worst possible crooks and murderers.

But Greenlands was worse for lawlessness than when he had last known it. There were grim events nightly, and yet the town was supposed to have law and order. When the rannigans from outlying ranches rode into town for a spree and started fights leading to shootings – and men were killed and hurt – it was more than just the way of the west. It was not the boisterous gunplay that jagged Jack Griffin's sense of law and order, it was the undercurrent of crookedness that held certain leading inhabitants that griped him.

He had heard strange tales about villainy and certain men. He knew that Sheriff Tom Mortimer was getting old. He seemed to be averse to cleaning up. Maybe it wasn't just age with Tom. Jack Griffin really did not know – but he was suspicious.

'I'll have to buy me that spread,' muttered Jack as his horse jogged along. 'I'll have to mind my own business. Ain't nothin' to me if Ern Spiceland has got cows that don't belong to him! Though I never figured Ern to be a rustler. Not the short time I've known him. And, if Sam Brant goes an' gets himself shot up – is that my business? Sure figure I'll buy me that Box-T spread at the far end of the plain – and buy me a good hoss! This hired hack ain't for me.'

He could only conclude he had taken on the job of lawman through sheer force of habit. He had spent three years chasing badmen and had some bad moments which he would prefer to forget. Death dealing wasn't so funny. But maybe he could spend a little more time with the law until he was ready to buy that ranch and forget gun-play.

There was really little incentive money-wise for a man to become a deputy except the urge to take sides with the law.

It was a good hour later when Jack Griffin rode his horse into Greenlands. The town lay under the afternoon heat, with a few loungers taking it easy in front of the saloons. An occasional buckboard rattled through the dusty main drag, and a lone rider caked with sweat and dust rode tiredly along the street.

Jack urged his mount up to the sheriff's office. He was grim and his head still ached. He walked in and went down a passage, his boots making clumping sounds on the bare boards. He came to the office which served Tom Mortimer as a home from home. He expected to find the rugged old-timer sitting at the desk, fooling with papers. But Tom was not in the office.

Jack looked around, puzzled. He went over to a bench at the rear of the big room where he found some water in a jug. He washed the bruise on his head. Then he went into the living-room of the building and looked around for sign of Sam Brant.

'Odd,' he muttered. 'I thought that galoot could not be moved!'

He was suddenly wary. He had left the deputy sheriff a badly wounded man. Tom Mortimer and Bertram Wast had been attending him. Yet Sam Brant was not in the bed in the living-room where he had last seen him.

Still puzzled, a bit fed up with events, Jack returned to the tie-rail and got his horse. He figured to go along to the Red Pine saloon. He might find Tom Mortimer there.

Jack rode the horse slowly to the garish saloon and dismounted. Three men on the verandah of the Red

Pine stared at Jack and he tried to grin back at them. The men made no comment as he walked to the batwing doors, although one man did flick his eyes over the deputy badge which Jack still wore on his shirt.

He pushed through the doors and stopped. He fumbled in his shirt pocket for the 'makings', giving himself time to think. He saw Tom Mortimer sitting at a table with another man.

'Ern got away, Tom,' drawled Jack and he stared down at the two men.

Sheriff Tom Mortimer stared at the younger man from under busy eyebrows. 'Got away! Well, I thought I told you to bring him in.'

'He knocked me off my hoss.'

The other man looked displeased. 'Huh! You were bested. Did you fight?'

'Wasn't any fightin' to mention. I just got a bump on the head. Ern rode off. Maybe he's back on his spread. I don't know. All I want to say is I've changed my mind about being a deputy, Tom. I came to Greenlands to settle down, buy me a spread. I shouldn't have ridden out after Ern Spiceland. I don't even know why you want him.'

'I've told you, Jack.' Tom Mortimer bluffed, looking worriedly at Bertram Wast. He stroked his black moustache as if he was anxious about something.

'So you couldn't keep a hombre by your side,' mocked the big man in store clothes who sat with Tom Mortimer.

Jack looked down warily at Bertram Wast. This man was the wealthy owner of the big Bar-K outfit. This was the gent who, only five years ago, had arrived at Greenlands, a stranger with money. Now, due to clever manipulations of loans, he owned most of the range around the town and the cattle. Not until a man rode more than half a day did he sight the land of other ranchers in the county. The rumours said that Wast had managed most of his prosperity by cunning moves, bringing in loans, downright hardness unknown previously in the area. And maybe some hidden crookedness, but that could not be substantiated.

'Maybe I was too blamed friendly,' admitted Jack. 'I sure did not expect Ern to bang into me – an' I sure as hell didn't figure to bang my head on something hard and lose my senses. But you haven't explained much, Tom. You just said that Ern had cows on his spread that didn't belong there. You didn't say if those cows had worked-over brands or had just strayed.'

'Strayed nothing!' snapped Bertram Wast. 'I'll tell you, Griffin, those longhorns on Spiceland's ranch are Bar-K cattle. Maybe some of them have worked-over brands. Did you look hard, Griffin?'

'I looked, Mister Wast.'

'We won't know until some guy with some sense takes a good look at 'em. And they couldn't be strays because this Spiceland galoot is busy fencing his east boundary. He's got wire an' posts fixed up.'

'You're sure well informed, Mister Wast. You know more than me. Maybe Ern is just fencin' his water-holes, huh?'

'Some lawman you aim to be!' jeered Wast.

Jack Griffin stared at Tom Mortimer. 'Anyway, I'm tellin' you, Tom, I'm not the deputy sheriff any more. There's too many things I don't rightly understand and you ain't explaining.'

The sheriff did not look at Jack. Instead, he reached savagely for his drink and gulped it.

'What happened to Sam Brant? I don't figure he got up and walked away.'

'You're blamed right he didn't. He died. He's buried right now.'

Jack blew cigarette smoke for some time before replying. 'Mighty fast trip to Boothill. He was suffering from lead poisoning, I know, but I didn't figure he'd die.'

'Wal, he did – plumb quick. So we buried him, same as we'd do for anyone else.'

'Reckon that makes Mike Capstaff a murderer.' He stared intently at the two men. Jack's eyes were watching the slight twitches on the faces of the other guys. 'Because that wasn't fair gun-play.'

'We'll get him,' growled Tom Mortimer, and he glanced anxiously at Bertram Wast.

Jack saw the quick look and he wondered why Tom was so worried about placating the wealthy owner of the Bar-K.

Jack Griffin began to unclip the deputy badge from his shirt. Tom Mortimer rose suddenly and put out a detaining hand. 'Wear that badge a mite longer, friend. I need a deputy. The problems of law and order in this blamed town are getting worse.'

'Then maybe you'll get around to explainin' more about Ern Spiceland? Why are you so suspicious of him?'

'I'll explain, sure thing, young feller,' said the old-timer hurriedly. 'Just you keep that badge nice an' visible.'

Jack fastened it again, slowly, very deliberately, and then without another word he walked to the bar. He ordered a drink from the fat attendant behind the mahogany. As he stood at the counter, he was wondering how Tom Mortimer could justify accusation against Ern Spiceland. There didn't seem to be much evidence so far.

Jack was a tall lean man. Under the black gaberdine shirt iron-hard muscles rippled, the product of hard riding and many other activities. One gun lay low on his right thigh, in a dark shiny holster that had seen some wear. He was wearing blue jeans over which were leather bat-wing chaps. There was nothing fanciful nor ornamental about his holster belt but he did wear leather cuffs just above the wrists which were studded with gleaming brass, quite effective as western gear. His grey Stetson capped dark wiry hair gave him some authority. His eyes were often very blue against his sun-reddened face.

The saloon was not very busy, for most of the cow-hands were out on the distant spreads, but a few rannigans were propped up against the bar. Jack did not know any of them. There were some he wouldn't want to know in any circumstances. In a corner a gambler in a black suit played a straight-faced game with a rancher who seemingly had had more than enough of the raw whiskey.

Jack turned figuring it was time he went back to his hotel. He waved to Tom Mortimer. He did not make any gesture to Bertram Wast. There was something about the man he did not like. He felt some strange antagonism towards the man, something that could not be explained. Maybe it was the rumours he had heard during the few weeks he had been back in town. Maybe this dislike of the galoot was something physical, something about the fellow's appearance. These feelings were difficult to define.

Jack rode his nag along to the livery, paid the stableman for the hire and strolled out. He felt damned hungry. Maybe he needed a slap-up meal of steak and kidney pie and plenty of coffee. His own custom-built saddle and other gear were in his room at the hotel. He began to stroll back to the Packhorse Hotel and then he heard the sound of gunshots in the warm afternoon air.

Colt gunshots did not figure as anything unusual in a town like Greenlands, where men used weapons as toys, when they were not being deadly earnest. Jack started back to the Red Pine saloon, sensing that was the area of the shots. Even as he sighted the saloon, a man hurtled out with long strides and jumped to a waiting horse. Even as he rowelled the animal cruelly, he snapped two more random shots at the batwing doors. The rider was moving swiftly down the main drag before two men spilled from the bar and leaped to horses in order to make chase.

Jack rushed to the batwings, still aware that he was a lawman. He was of course on foot. He rushed into the saloon, unsure of what he would find.

The shots could be some waddies making free with lead, but who was the guy in such a hurry to leave? He hadn't recognised the man as anyone he knew.

He went into the saloon, wary, angry and alert, his hand near his Colt .45. On the floor of the saloon lay the body of a man and around it clustered a few men. As Jack strode forward, he saw Bertram Wast, leaning over the body. Jack lunged forward and glanced grimly over Wast's shoulder. Jack started into the contorted face of Tom Mortimer.

A slug had shattered a hole in the sheriff's heart and blood spurted to the bare boards of the saloon floor. There was the smell of death, a grimness in the air.

'Who did it?' snapped Jack Griffin.

Bertram Wast rose to his feet, dark eyes meeting

Jack's blue ones in real antagonism. Then the man dusted his hands as if there was nothing more final than death. 'It was Mike Capstaff.'

'That hombre again!' Jack looked at the others questioningly. 'Sure?'

'Sure we're sure!' Wast sneered.

'He came in like a galoot who's sure lookin' for gunplay,' rasped the fat bartender.

'Sure was,' drawled another range-rider. 'The sheriff went for his smoke-pole but that hellion was too fast.'

'Why should that owl-hoot kill old Tom?'

Bertram Wast seemed to have ready answers, another quality Jack did not like in the man. 'Seems like Tom Mortimer and Sam Brant got on the wrong side o' Mike Capstaff.'

Jack Griffin was caustic. 'Couldn't one of you hombres put a slug in that outlaw's belly? I reckon you had time.'

'He sure made a fast play,' growled the beer slinger. 'I ain't no gun-hand. That jigger was in an' out in a matter of seconds. I guess he had a hoss waiting.'

'Yeah — that figures,' snapped Jack. 'I don't suppose he had a railroad ticket! Hope those two fellers after him hit him with some lead. At least someone wanted to try.'

Bertram Wast picked up his unfinished drink from the table at which he had so recently sat with the sheriff. He drank it off as if a gesture. He even smacked his lips. 'Wal, I guess this town needs a new sheriff.'

'Wait! Are you forgetting I'm the deputy?' Jack spat the words out, as if to confront this man.

Wast stopped at the batwings. His dark strong face was questioning.

'I figured you were turning the job in,' he said, a big man in his black store suit. Jack wondered fleetingly if the man packed a gun, not that there was any hint of a weapon. But the rancher could carry a small derringer somewhere under his voluminous coat.

Jack Griffin touched the badge on his shirt, looking down at the prone body. When his eyes flicked at the others again in the saloon, his face was grim, as if there were hidden decisions stirring in his mind. Two more curious men came through the batwings and stared around.

'Tom was a good feller,' said Jack. 'Maybe he made mistakes like all of us an' maybe he was getting old for the job. He sure seemed to me like a hombre with troubles on his conscience – but maybe I'm wrong. Anyway he swore me in as deputy and I'll keep on with the job in the meantime. In fact, if you want a full-time sheriff I'll stand for the job until I get me a ranch to handle.'

'Judge Tarrant, over in Abilene, is the gent who'll decide on a new sheriff for Greenlands,' drawled Bertram Wast. 'That is after he listens to local folk.'

'Like you, huh?'

'Maybe. I know his town and surrounding territory limits.'

'Guess I'll abide by the judge's opinions,' drawled Jack.

'That's mighty good of you,' sneered Wast. 'Maybe I'll inform the judge of that, huh?'

Jack Griffin moved over to the batwing doors. Doc Turner, who was also the town's undertaker, was examining the dead body with some professional interest. 'Nothin' but shootings in this burg. If I patch 'em up, they got to pay me. If I put 'em in a casket, the town's funds got to pay. Figure I can't lose anyway!'

Grimly, Jack went among the cow-men and townsfolk who had gathered outside the saloon to discuss the killing, and he got three men to agree to ride after the other two who had chased Mike Capstaff. The two men climbed to horses immediately and Jack gave them a last word.

'I figure that owl-hooter is hard to find as soon as he hits the hills. But you can try to find his trail an' if so let me know. Reckon I'll stick here an' look into Tom's desk. Might pick up a clue about things in general.'

There was a big query in the situation. Why had Mike Capstaff journeyed into town and shot Sam Brant and Tom Mortimer? At first the killing of Sam Brant had passed like an accidental clash, an outlaw meeting a lawman. But the man had returned and murdered the sheriff. There seemed, now, to be deliberate intent behind it all.

Jack went along to the Packhorse Hotel and climbed to the second floor where he had rented a room. Inside, he opened a saddle pack. He brought out a holster belt and slowly strapped it around his waist. He adjusted it until the shiny holster hung low on his left thigh and matched the one on his right side. Then he brought another Colt out of the pack. He examined the weapon, saw it was working easily and then he loaded it with shells. He slipped it into the empty holster. Now he felt just like old times when he had hunted men, lawless rannigans with a price on their heads.

'Two guns are better than one,' he muttered. 'For a galoot who is used to matching Colts!'

He made his way to the street and walked along to

the sheriff's office. Now that there was no actual sheriff of Greenlands, he figured he was in charge. A reluctant lawman! Strange how events worked out!

In the office, he began to look through the odd documents that Tom Mortimer had kept, mostly in some disorder.

But he found nothing which would throw light on Tom's intention to question Ern Spiceland about rustled cattle on his spread. It sure seemed that Tom kept records in his head – and he was dead now.

Jack leafed through some old descriptions of wanted men, rannigans on the run. There was nothing about Mike Capstaff, so there was no clue here.

He lunged impatiently to the street again, feeling he had to do something damned decisive about these killings. He'd get back to his old grim ways of dealing with dangerous men. He made his way to the livery. There was one thing he really needed if he was going to dive back into the role of gunhand and that was a good horse which he could call his own.

When he had landed in Greenlands a few weeks ago, he had come in on the stage which ran from the railroad head at Abilene some thirty miles away. And from that date he had hired a nag for the small amount of riding he had so far done.

In the livery, he found the proprietor. A few words and he was led to the stall where he had last seen the big roan. He had noticed the animal earlier, knew he could have some affinity with the crittur. He ran hands over the flanks of the tall proud horse, breathed close to the animal's nostrils and saw the response in the eyes.

'I'd like to buy this cayuse.'

'Sure. Make me an offer.'

Five minutes later he had gotten his saddle, bedroll, lariat and rifle from out of his room at the Packhorse Hotel. The feel of leather seemed like old times. He was glad he had hauled it all the way down the railroad and the final stage. He rigged the roan quickly and pushed the rifle into the saddle holster. Then he rode out of the livery. The proud animal responded nicely. Some man had treated the crittur with respect in the past. The horse seemed to like its new owner. The affinity was there already.

Jack rode slowly along with the intention of trying out his new mount later on some open range. He suddenly saw the stage rattle in with a pounding of hoofs and a cloud of dust. This was the daily trip from Abilene.

As he rode alongside, curious like the rest of the townspeople, he saw a girl alight. She was about the third passenger to get off and he noted a young fellow assisted her to the dusty street.

The girl was dressed in a long coat of corduroy which had a natural swing from a beautifully feminine waist. Some quality in the lithe body held Jack's eyes, making him smile. He realised with the impact of a bullet hitting a tree how little a lovely woman had featured in his harsh life.

Under her hat corn-coloured hair rioted. There was something set in her expression but that did not detract from the truth that this creature was a beauty. But who was the galoot helping her alight? Something about him reminded Jack of Ern Spiceland – but that was surely just coincidence?

Jack Griffin jigged his roan closer. The young man was something of a dandy, in a light suit which had obviously been made in an eastern city. To match it, he wore a dark hat and a black necktie.

Jack Griffin threw his reins over a nearby hitching-rail and moved closer to the girl and the young newcomer. For some moments he stared thoughtfully while luggage was being handed down from the stage. Then, coming closer, he spoke up. 'I'm the deputy sheriff, name of Jack Griffin, now acting as sheriff. Care to tell me your name, mister?'

The young fellow turned, his eyes so like Ern Spiceland's. 'Sure. Why not? In fact, you're just the man we want to see. I'm Fred Spiceland, Ern's brother, and this is my sister, Jane. Just yesterday we heard that Ern was in trouble and we've come right over to see him.'

'He rode out.'

'I hear Ern tangled with the sheriff. Is that right, Mister Griffin?'

'Wal, yeah, sort of. But I can straighten it out in time, I guess. Trouble is there's been some killings.'

'Oh? Who was so unfortunate?'

'Tom Mortimer, the sheriff, for one – an' the deputy, Sam Brant, for another. An owl-hoot by the name of Mike Capstaff killed the sheriff. But it's a bit of a long story.'

'Oh, how I hate to hear about killings and downright murder!' exclaimed the girl. 'Life should be precious!'

'Wal, it ain't,' said Jack quietly. 'Not out here, the way the west is right now. Maybe some day, huh?'

'I can't believe that Ern would rustle cattle,' went on the girl in great indignation.

'How did you hear all this?'

'A friend came in on the morning stage to Abilene, the special run,' Fred Spiceland seemed anxious to explain. 'Seems the news circulated around this town the moment you rode out. What happened, deputy – or should I address you as sheriff?'

'I'm a lawman right now.' Jack touched his badge. Again he could hardly take his appreciative gaze off the girl, and she noticed because she actually began to blush!

'As I say, Ern rode out.'

'He ran away? Not like my brother,' cried the girl.

'I knew Ern and liked him. But I was the deputy and had to ride after him. Trouble is, he bested me.'

'Oh? How?'

'He knocked me flying offen my cayuse,' admitted Jack Griffin. 'I doubt if he is at his ranch right now – but maybe I'm wrong.'

'He won't run away like some law-breakers!' gasped Jane. 'Not my elder brother! How can you criticise him if you're his friend?'

'I'm carrying a law-badge.' Jack hated to argue with this lovely girl but it seemed she was pushing him. 'These are the facts. An owl-hoot by the name of Mike Capstaff murdered Tom Mortimer, the sheriff. An' Sam Brant, the deputy before me, was shot by the same mean devil. I had to go out and get Ern for questioning but he sure tricked me, I've gotta admit. I don't know where he is right now. But I promise you that Ern will get a fair hearin' as long as I'm the law around here – but that might not be for ever because I might be sacked. I'm not satisfied with the allegations concerning your brother, miss, and I'm plumb mad about these recent killings. Shouldn't damned happen even in a town like Greenlands, but murder is a fact of life around here. I aim to discover why these men were killed. There has to be reasons. Got all that, Mister Spiceland?'

'Sure, sure. But call me Fred.'

'As soon as we can change, we're riding out to Ern's ranch,' said the girl wih great determination.

Jack nodded. As he turned, two range-hands rode into the dusty street and wearily dismounted close to the stage. One man clutched a red wound in his shoulder and almost fell from his horse. Jack recognised the two galoots as the men who had earlier went riding after Mike Capstaff.

'Bad luck,' said one man grimly. 'My hoss went lame and Bud here stopped some lead that blamed owlhoot flung at us. Had to turn back.'

'Okay – you tried.'

'I saw the other three fellers ridin' out in chase but they'll never catch Mike Capstaff. He'll hit the hills.'

'Yeah.'

'An' they should go easy. That mean bastard is a killer!'

2
Battle at Round-O

Jack Griffin was standing ouside the Packhorse Hotel some fifteen minutes later, waiting to see Jane Spiceland and her brother. He had his roan all set for a late ride, knowing he'd had a full stint of riding activity already. He figured to ride out with the girl and Fred and try to get to the bottom of the rustling allegations against Ern. He was agreeably surprised when he saw Jane. She had changed from her city clothes to range garb. She looked like a slim youth in some ways, although not entirely because she was undoubtedly feminine. She wore blue jeans tucked into riding boots, and a red shirt and yellow bandanna caught his eyes. Then he noticed the fair hair under the fawn Stetson and thought she was the most beautiful female in town.

'I'll ride over with you,' Jack announced.

'That's kind of you.'

'He might go off at the sight of me, though. You can reassure him – if we actually see him.'

Fred was still wearing his city suit but he had got himself some high-heel cowboy boots and his pants were tucked into them.

'I want to see Ern,' said Jack. 'If he's still around.'

'Why shouldn't he be around?' asked Jane.

'Wal, I'm the law an' he hit me mighty hard with his big fist, and to be mighty candid he did leave me kinda alone out there in the Panhandle. But maybe I'll forget all that if he can do some explaining. I want to know why he was afraid to come into town with me.'

'There are plenty of things we want to understand,' said the girl indignantly.

'Ern was always in trouble,' said Fred. 'I'm the youngest, you know. Do you figure I look more than nineteen, Mister Griffin?'

Jack smiled. 'Maybe. What do you work at back in Abilene?'

'I'm studying to be a lawyer. Plenty of scope for a trained man out here. Jane teaches. She's good with the kids.'

Some ten minutes later all three rode out of Greenlands, with a high sun on their backs. The land around the town was good for cattle for miles, with plenty of tufted grasses, hence the name Greenlands. But out on the flat Panhandle heat shimmers distorted the horizon and the grass was yellowed although still holding nourishment for wandering cattle. In the far distance they could see the dull blurs of the rising hills. This broken country was the location of Ern's Round-O ranch, poor land for cattle. The longhorns had to move around constantly to find fresh grassy tufts among the mesquite and catclaw.

The foothills marked the western end of the Panhandle plain. In that area the floors of the numerous canyons were sandy and full of scrub. The appearance of Joshua trees and other giant cactus was proof that the land tended to be dry and poor.

It was late afternoon when they rode closer to Ern

Spiceland's ranch. Then the house and pole corrals became visible and they saw bunches of steers that shied away nervously at the approach of horses. Jack got a view of the Round-O brand worked into their hides. So far as he could see, there were no worked-over brands but of course it was difficult to look for every steer belonging to Ern Spiceland. The way he figured it, Ern would be crazy to try to alter the brands. That was not an easy proposition. So how had the accusation stuck?

Jack Griffin was way ahead of Jane and her young brother when he heard the sudden crack of Colts being fired and then a rifle spat with its deeper noise. He rowelled his roan and the animal sprang instantly and almost gladly. He knew he was going to like this crittur. They'd be as one.

There was a defined trail leading to the ranch-house. He had ridden that way earlier and everything looked just the same, and then he saw the lurking men fire guns at the house.

There were no cottonwoods to give shade as in the case of many typical spreads. The buildings lay in a slight hollow. Suddenly he noticed the figures of men hiding near the barn. The attackers!

He realised he was the only one with guns. Fred and Jane were not the type to carry weapons. He eased out the Colt from his holster on his right side. He realised he might be glad of two loaded guns, apart from his rifle. The roan's hoofs beat a rapid tattoo on the dry earth and then the horse cleared a pole fence at its rider's command and came up behind the barn. Jack began to fire as soon as he roan steadied after the jump.

He had seen some answering fire from the ranch-house and he figured out that Ern Spiceland was there using his guns.

The two men wheeled at his swift approach, obviously not anticipating trouble. But they crouched and fired. Their hand-gun slugs whistled past his head and only served to annoy Jack Griffin. The hell with this! Damn them! He had not survived umpteen encounters with badmen just to go down because of two cowardly gunhands!

Jack sat the saddle, thighs gripping the rib-cage of the big roan, and his hardware was out from both holsters and snapping fast shots at the two men. Even the strong roan jibbed in fright at this activity and a slug tore at his hat. That made Jack grimace in distaste. Good hats cost money! But it was sure better than a hole in his crust!

As his horse jibbed and wheeled, the movement made him a difficult target even if it added to his troubles in aiming. Shots began to sing through the air in all directions. All at once, one of the attackers pitched forward like a dummy, going flat down to the earth and staying there. Jack figured the galoot had stopped some lead! So here was one dead man already, he figured grimly. As for the other gunny, he darted a desperate glance to right and left and went leaping around the barn in an effort to run away. So much for this man's bravado with a weapon!

Jack reloaded one Colt quickly. He had a pocket full of shells, a habit from the old days. He jigged his horse after the man. The leathers were slack around the horse's neck, the animal responding nicely to the pressure of Jack's knees.

In this manner man and horse edged around the barn enabling Jack to take a pot-shot at the escaping gunny. At once the guy clutched his arm and howled in pain. Sure, this guy was no hero. Then the man darted around a big stack of logs.

There came the sound of hoofs and Jack realised the man had jumped to a cayuse hidden behind the logs. He was about to go after him in these split seconds of activity when something else swiftly claimed his attention.

Apparently there were three attacking ruffians for all at once another man rode around the ranch-house. His horse was dragging a chain to which was attached a big bundle of blazing tree branches. Swiftly, the man urged his horse up to the gable-end of the ranch-house and bringing the blazing wood close to the building, an old Indian trick if ever there was one. There were no windows at that side and Ern Spiceland could not see the man. Even as Jack Griffin urged his big roan to a better angle, the man cast off the drag chain and spurred his animal cruelly.

Jack did trigger off some fast shots at the escaping man but the rannigan had the devil's own luck. He seemed to be unhit.

Jack had to choose between shooting and doing something about the blazing wood. He leaped from the roan and began to kick the blazing branches away in a flurry of bright sparks. Already the brands had charred the side of the ranch-house. It seemed the burning wood had been dipped in some inflammable substance, which meant that these three ruffianly range-riders had done some planning.

For some minutes Jack Griffin was involved in frantic kicking and stamping at the burning bale of wood. He got the main part clear. Soon it was under control and at that moment he was aware that he had been joined by the others. Then he saw Ern Spiceland's bright eyes and swarthy face beside him.

'These skunks wanted to burn you out, Ern!'

'Yeah. An' they kinda wanted me dead, too. They're Bar-K men.'

'Bertram Wast's hands! You sure?'

'Come around and see the hombre you plugged.'

He walked away, a tall lean figure in flapping chaps and vest. Jack went after him, dusting the burnt charcoal from his hands. Fred and Jane moved after their brother, so far no exchange of greetings or explanations.

The dead man was a hairy-looking animal in dirty range gear. Jack's slug had taken him between the eyes, splashing blood over the face until it was a mask. Jack stared in distaste.

'In spite of the slug spoiling his looks,' said Ern, 'I know this hombre. He is Jed Slacks. Worked for Wast.'

'Can't say I know him,' muttered Jack. 'But that means little seeing I've only been back here a short time.' He turned to Ern. 'Now, look, friend – what's going on? How come these galoots are trying to burn you out?'

'I don't know.'

'Aw, heck, Ern, what sort of answer is that?'

'I tell you I just don't know why. But I know who is trying to get me outa this ranch.'

'Who, for cryin' out aloud?'

'Bertram Wast.'

'But he's got the biggest ranch in this part of the Panhandle. Why should that feller try to get you out o' the Round-O?'

'I've just told you, I don't know.'

Ern Spiceland glanced at his brother and sister and grinned. 'Hey, you two! How come you're ridin' out with the deputy?'

'We heard some stories.'

'Sure, Ern. Guess we haven't seen you for a long time.' Fred nodded.

'Wal, you can see me now. Tom Mortimer ain't gettin' me in his lock-up.' Ern swung to Jack. 'Wast is trying to pin somethin' on me. I ain't put an iron to one of his steers. My longhorns are my own, Griffin. Maybe I should have told you this instead of ramming fists at you. But I figured you were working for Tom Mortimer and Wast. I thought it was crazy for me to ride into town for Wast to frame me.'

'You can count Tom Mortimer out now,' said Jack.

'How come? That old galoot has sure got himself under Wast's little finger.'

'He's dead, Ern. Mike Captaff walked into the Red Pine and drilled him.'

'Hell!' Ern found it hard to say anything for a few moments. Then: 'Wast had Tom Mortimer just like that.' Ern made a gesture with his fingers. 'I can't prove anythin'. Figure it out for yourself, Griffin. Mike Capstaff didn't salivate the sheriff for nothin'. And it were no accident Sam Brant got plugged like you told me. Nope, no accident – that's all I kin say!'

'Sam Brant is more than just plugged, Ern. He's dead.'

'Dead! I'm right, Griffin. Someone's plotting. An' I know who.'

They walked around to the front of the ranch-house. The house was mill-cut timber for there were few trees for miles around in the Panhandle area. The modest little place had a stone-built chimney rising on one gable end. As they went on to the verandah, Ern turned and scanned the horizon.

'That bandy rannigan who works for me ought to be back from Greenlands,' he muttered. 'Anyways, set yourselves in and I'll get some chow. Guess you could do with some coffee, Jane.'

But the girl was near the stove already. 'I may be a school-marm but I can cook, and if I remember rightly, your coffee is so black it nearly chokes me.'

While the three were talking and getting ready to drink and eat, Jack Griffin went out to the verandah again. He was grimly puzzled. He was beginning to realise that there was some deep play going on. If the dead man had been in Bertram Wast's employ, there was some explaining to be done by the owner of the Bar-K. Of course Wast would disclaim any responsibility but that would not obviate the need for inquiries to be made. And as deputy sheriff the task would fall to him. Already he was up against Bertram Wast. But why should the Bar-K owner, with his vast spread, desire to force Ern Spiceland off his poor ranch?

While Jack pondered the problems, he noticed a cloud of trail dust rising on the horizon. Slowly the cloud came nearer until he could distinguish the buckboard and horses responsible for the dust. The outfit came on at a good lick and finally rattled into the ranch-yard. A thick-set little man came waddling up to Jack.

'Howdy, Deputy. I'm Bandy Manners – work for Ern. I'm a goldarned cook, swamper and puncher rolled into one. Not that I get more pay! Huh! Heh! You here to arrest Ern again?'

'I ain't arresting anyone – yet.'

'You got sense.' The little man figured that was a shrewd remark and chuckled again.

As they turned to go inside the ranch-house, Jack remarked: 'I figure I might want that buckboard, Bandy.'

'Why? Huh?'

'I want to take a dead man to Greenlands.'

'Dead man! Say, who's dead now?'

Jack Griffin told him and jerked a hand to indicate the side of the ranch-house where they had left the body.

'Bar-K hombre, huh?' grunted Bandy Manners. 'That's bad. Wast won't like that.'

'You know of any good reason why Wast should make a play to get Ern outa this ranch?'

'Nary an idee!'

'D'you figure Wast wants this spread for some reason – some way-out idea?'

'I just figger Wast wouldn't let a jack-rabbit live. He is tryin' to run Ern off this range, sure thing. I've seen Bar-K riders up in the foothills. Ern has filed a claim on all that land.'

'What were the riders doing exactly?'

'Nuthin' so far as I could see. Just ridin' around. I couldn't figure out why.'

Jack Griffin had to 'set to' with the others and enjoy the rough hospitality offered by Ern Spiceland with the assistance of Jane, and for an active man good food was always welcome. There was plenty of beans, bacon and coffee. 'Thanks for the grub,' said Jack and added wryly: 'I can now forget about that bang on the head!'

'Think nothing of it,' grinned Ern.

But there was work to do. 'I'm deputy sheriff, Ern, and I've got to look around the spread, take a look at your beef. Wast makes allegations and so I've just got to investigate. I figure we could ride around and take a good look at your stock.'

'You're welcome – an' you're wasting your time. But I'll be glad to show you around. If there are any Bar-K cattle on my range, they are strays.'

'I'll be lookin' for worked-over brands.'

'You won't find any.'

Bandy Manners was bristling with indignation as he listened but he subsided after some minutes. He realised that Jack had to be impartial.

They set off a little later, leaving the ranch in charge of Bandy Manners. Jane was not deterred from going with the men alhough Ern warned her they would have to complete a good two hours of hard riding. There was just time to ride around part of the ranch and look at some stock and then get back to Greenlands before the sun vanished in a red blaze in the west. They wanted to avoid night riding.

They found some longhorns way out on the plain. The four riders hazed the cattle into a group and then Jack went around examining the brands. It was necessarily swift work. He found the steers were all clearly Round-O stock. They rode away into the rising buttes of the broken, almost arid, land. Ern had said there were some small herds in the canyons, foraging for spare grass. Many cattle followed a lead steer. Ern was quite willing to show Jack Griffin as much stock as possible in the limited time.

They rode into the mesquite-covered floor of a small canyon. A bunch of cows were nosing through the vegetation at the far end. The lean longhorns lifted heads as the riders approached but they could not get out of the canyon, although they tried to lumber away at the approach of the intruders.

Jack Griffin's attitude was merely that of a man doing his duty. He liked the Spicelands. Bertram Wast had made accusations and so the matter must be settled. The job had been Tom Mortimer's. How much had Tom believed in the accusations?

The beef was hazed into a bunch by Ern and Fred, and Jack went among the bawling cattle to examine the brands. It was mostly a question of a quick glance but he would try not to miss one animal. If he was satisfied in his own mind he could reply to Bertram Wast with confidence and put that man in his place.

And then, suddenly, he saw the Bar-K band with a worked over Round-O. The superimposed brand was badly done. Usually in a case of rustling, where altered brands were concerned, cattle with old brands were selected. The old brand was then roughed out altogether and a new brand burned deeply. But with this Texas longhorn the Round-O brand had been clumsily burned over the old Bar-K marks, making the whole thing obvious to anyone at first sight.

With a grave face Jack pointed at the animal. The others saw his gesture. Ern's face darkened grimly.

There were other longhorns in the herd similarly worked over. Jack Griffin counted ten animals in the small bunch that had probably followed a lead steer into the canyon. And those longhorns all bore the clumsily-altered brands.

Jack rode out of the herd, gestured to Ern to follow, and they went down the area a little way from the bawling cattle. Fred and Jane followed, wondering.

Jack leaned forward with his hands on the addle horn. 'How do you figure that beef got there?'

Ern Spiceland was angry. 'Listen, Jack, you can see with your own eyes that this is a setup. These brands are fakes.'

'Well –'

'You think I'd do this?' shouted Ern, his old temper rising.

'Give me time to answer, will yuh! No – I don't, but –'

'Do you think I'd bring you along to look at stolen cattle? Do you think I knew about these longhorns?'

'Are they your cattle, Ern?'

'No, by Gawd! Now ask me who altered those damned brands!'

'I sure will. Who altered them, Ern?'

'As sure as all hell it wasn't me, Mister Deputy! But I can guess. Wast had the cattle worked over and then herded them on to my range. He's tryin' to pin something on me. He wants me off this land for some almighty important reason.'

'You say they are not your beef,' commented Jack. 'You didn't buy them? You haven't a bill of sale?'

'I got no bill of sale an' I didn't buy them off Wast or any other jasper!' said Ern violently.

Jack gave a tight-lipped grin. 'Keep your hair on, Ern. I'm only askin' questions. The way I see it you're framed pretty nicely by some jasper. Wast has only to lead a posse of men from town to take a looksee at these critturs and you know the general conclusion would be that you rustled 'em and altered the brand marks. The cattlemen around here don't like rustlers. There was a bit of that in the past and it caused a fair rumpus.'

Ern shifted grimly in his saddle and flashed a glance at his brother and sister. They were quiet, realising this situation needed sorting out.

'How come you don't believe I've stolen this beef?' Ern jerked his question at the deputy.

'Because only a blamed fool would leave them in this canyon so near to your ranch. A real rustler hides the critturs — or sells 'em off so darned fast they move like ghosts!'

'Thanks!'

'If you'd known the cows were here, you wouldn' have brought me along to find them. I can see the circumstances are against you, Ern. And I can also see the facts that are in your favour. But if Wast wants to work up something, he sure could make it stick. I wonder how long these brutes have been here?'

Ern moved his head, glancing at the wide sweep of the mesquite in the canyon. 'Day or two most likely, by the look of the grass – or what's left of it. I ain't been thisaway myself for more than a week.'

Jack Griffin raised his head and looked at the dying sun. 'Let's get going. Nothing we can do about these longhorns tonight.'

'What the heck can I do about them in any case?'

'You can do plenty when we find the galoots who altered these brands – and I figure Wast will know the identity of those men.'

Ern slapped a fist into the palm of his other hand. 'Sure. That would prove the whole thing a blamed fake!'

'That won't be easy,' warned Jack.

'You ain't arrestin' me?' Ern grinned. 'No hassle?'

Jack grinned at Jane. 'No arrests today. I don't want another bang on the head – that right, Jane?'

'You're the lawman.'

Jack jigged his horse forward. 'Maybe I can find out who actually did this fake branding. That won't be easy.'

'You'd have to stick a knife into a villain before he'd talk,' growled Ern.

'Money makes men talk – but dollars don't grow like cactus.'

They turned the horses and rode slowly out of the canyon, the sinking sun on their backs. They were all deep in thought until they got near to the Round-O ranch. When they rode into the yard Bandy Manners came forward to greet them. He had the dead man loaded on to the buckboard.

'You want me to drive this dead 'un into town?' he

yelled at Jack Griffin.

'Nope. I'll take the loan of the buckboard an' drive this cadaver back into town myself. I don't want him up behind me on my saddle. Guess I don't like dead men behind me. I wan some honest citizens in town to identify this body as Wast's hired hand. My horse can follow on a lead. You and Ern got a job to do.'

'What's that?'

'Get those longhorns outa that canyon. Get them hidden somewheres in the hills. Remember I'm the deputy sheriff an' I didn't tell you this. It's unofficial. But get them beeves away somewhere so that Wast can't prove anythin' if he decides to bring some gents out to look at 'em. Wal, it's pretty certain Wast didn't heat the iron himself. In the meantime maybe I can get a clue as to who did the branding job.'

'Seems like good advice.'

Bandy Manners did not understand and had to be told about the cattle in the canyon. The little man's whiskers bristled in anger. 'Why, durn it, there's only me and Ern on this spread and you can take it from me we didn't put no iron to Bar-K cattle!'

'Right.' Jack whipped around. He glanced again admiringly at Jane. Then: 'You know what to do, Ern. Must be some place where those critturs can be hidden. It's a good move against a sudden trick by Wast. Because he knows the cattle are on your land. But if you hide them and he can't show them as evidence, you've beaten the man. Wal, I've got to take this stiff back for burial.'

Jack hitched the roan to the back of the buckboard and then climbed on board.

'We're staying in Greenlands for a day or two,' Jane called to her brother. 'We'll ride over some time. Maybe there is something we can do to help.'

'Sorry I can't put you up tonight,' Ern explained. 'But we've only got two bunks and even if Bandy and I slept somewheres else, the bunks are not good enough for you, Jane. Don't rightly know about you though, Fred. Want to stop the night?'

'Reckon I'd better go along with Jane.'

'Yeah – you mosey along. Take care of her, Fred.'

Jack jerked at the leathers and the buckboard rattled out of the dusty ranch yard. Jane and Fred followed on their hired nags. The little party soon left the Round-O spread and travelled swiftly towards the distant Greenlands.

When they entered the town the light from kerosene lamps sent straggling beams into the main drag. Jane and Fred said adios to Jack Griffin and went along to the hotel, tired and hungry after a long day. Jack had sterner duties.

He left the buckboard outside the sheriff's office and carried the dead man inside, grimly, like a sack of old spuds. Then he went along to get Doc Turner. The old medico man lived in a pretentious clap-board house at the end of the town. When Jack found him, he was drinking whiskey in his so-called surgery. He was not too pleased at being asked to go out and examine a corpse.

'Dead, huh? Can't he wait until morn? Never heard of a dead galoot who couldn't wait!'

'I want him certified dead, identified and then buried,' said Jack grimly.

Doc Turner peered at him over steel-rimmed spectacles. 'You ought to be sheriff, young man. All right, let's go.'

On the way back Jack stopped at a closed store. He knocked and soon collected another citizen. This was Al Bride, a storeman who knew everyone in the town, almost, and a lot from the outlying spreads. 'I want you to identify a dead hombre, Al. And I want you to certify him dead, Doc – which he sure is. It's all for the records. Once I've got them I can hand the body over to the grave-digger on Boothill. I've moved into the sheriff's office and I sure don't like bodies lyin' around.'

They tramped along the boardwalks and presently reached the brick wall of the lawman's office. Jack had left the door unlocked, following the free and easy custom of the days. They walked in, along the passage that flanked the living quarters, and then into the office.

Jack Griffin halted abruptly. He had left a corpse lying on the floor.

Right there and now here was no corpse! There was no body on the floor. And sure as heck that cadaver had not walked away!

Suddenly, brain flashing, he went swiftly to the cells, wondering if some guy had entered during his absence and played a joke. But the cells were bare. He wheeled and stared at the inquiring faces of Doc Turner and Al Bride. 'The body has gone! Someone's taken it.'

'Sure it couldn't ha' walked away?' joked Al Bride and a wide smile cracked the displeasure that had been on his face.

'Listen, man – the galoot was dead. Some bastard has been in here an' taken the cadaver away.'

'Stupid joke!'

'It's no joke,' snarled Jack, suspicions in his mind.

'Looky, Griffin,' rumbled Doc Turner, 'I'm getting to be an old man an' I don't like these chilly nights. Not after the heat of day. So good-night, sir. Find me that body tomorrow. Unless it has moseyed up Boothill an' buried iself.'

Doc Turner and the storekeeper went away, feeling that the matter was unimportant. But Jack knew there was some significance in the move. Someone had taken the dead man away and the reason was because that someone did not want the hombre identified.

He had a good idea who was responsible for the tricky move!

3
Bushwhackers Sometimes Die

Jack Griffin stood in the sheriff's office and thought it over for a moment, angry and a bit sour. Night was falling and indeed the sky would get darker. He was momentarily stumped. Of course Ern Spiceland had identified the dead man as Jed Slacks but Jack was keen to get a prominent citizen of Greenlands to testify to the man's identity and somehow link it with Bertram Wast.

'No damned cadaver!' he grunted to himself. 'They've pulled a fast one.'

It seemed that the entry of the buckboard into town had been noticed. Wast or his hands had worked quickly.

'They'll take that damned body out into the arid lands, put it in a hole and cover it up.' He was musing out aloud. 'All right – so I can't tackle Wast about his hired hands' attempt to burn Ern's ranch-house. But I can work on locating the crooks who rebranded those cows. But if Ern gets those cows nicely hidden, he sure has spoilt Wast's play.'

There was also the question of getting on to Mike

Capstaff's trail. And there was more to it than merely grabbing the outlaw – if he got the chance – and stringing him up for his crimes. He was duty-bound to learn just why Tom Mortimer and Sam Brant had been murdered. It was obvious that the outlaw had sought the two men and deliberately killed them. The reason why had to be a matter for the record, if nothing else.

Jack Griffin led the buckboard into an alley beside the office and then unhitched the horse. With his own roan, he led the animal along to the livery near the hotel.

Restless, he went back to the sheriff's office. He walked into the living quarters that had been used by Tom Mortimer. There was just a living-room with a bunk, simplicity indeed! Beyond that was a stove in a built-on recess. The quarters were clean and just as good as the room he had vacated in the Packhorse.

He dumped his saddle and bedroll in a corner and felt suddenly tired, grim, as if he had acquired worries. He examined his gun and checked for shells. He took off his hat and felt the bump on his head. The soreness was still there. For a moment he wondered why the hell he was bothering with all this hassle.

But he had an iron will which had taken him along many dangerous trails and he figured he would go on being stubborn. But he had never considered a man could dispense with sleep. A bit of shuteye might be a good idea. Tomorrow might bring a few more moves in this play.

But he locked the doors of the place. He used his own bedroll and got into the bunk after turning down the lamp. His gun-belt hung inches from his head.

He lay in the bunk, thinking that his plans to buy the

Box-T were going slightly astray. He was the hombre who had got tired of chasing bad men and yet here he was with the office of deputy sheriff and a bad tangle with lawbreakers. His plans for a quiet life as a rancher were not materialising.

So he fell asleep, thinking that when he finally bought his own spread and packed in the deputy job, it would be a fine thing for a man if he had a wife like, say, Jane Spiceland.

Next day, the early part of the morning was uneventful, except for a short talk with Jane, during which he told her how the body of Jed Slacks had disappeared. She was riding over with Fred to see her brother at the Round-O.

'I'll tell Ern what has happened,' she promised.

In a way he wished he could talk to her about more personal things, like the lovely way her eyes gleamed. But the words did not come easily.

Jack Griffin was standing on the boardwalk outside the lawman's office an hour later when Bertram Wast rode up with two of his hands. One man was Otto Tribe ramrod of the Bar-K. He was a lean, dark-eyed man with a knife scar fully six inches long down the side of his right cheek. He was more than a hard-driving ranch foreman. He was also a swift gun-hand by repute and as if wishing to substantiate his reputation he wore two Colts slung low in a fancy one-piece gun-belt, hardly the usual equipment of a cow-puncher ramrod.

The other man was a hefty-looking guy who could be any age past thirty. Jack knew he was completely bald under the floppy sombrero he wore. But he made up for this hirsute shortage with a big moustache which was startlingly red. So he was known as Red Holbin and had never been known as anything else since his arrival in town a year ago.

Jack knew the men. In a tough land they were pretty hard customers. He wheeled, stood with feet squarely apart and surveyed the men who sat their mounts. For their part they looked down at him almost insultingly.

'Mornin' Griffin,' called Bertram Wast with spurious cordiality.

The Bar-K owner did not look like a rancher. He wore his black suit and hat. Only his boots were the usual wear of a cattleman. His pants were folded into the long high-heeled boots. He did not carry a gun so far as Jack could see.

'Mornin', Wast,' Jack returned coldly.

Otto Tribe and Red Holbin sat in silence, leaning forward on their saddle horns, watching him.

'You heard the news?' asked Wast.

'What damned news?'

'Don't get leery. Judge Tarrant is coming over from Abilene by the afternoon stage and he's bringing a sheriff with him. A hombre by the name of Trick Grant.'

'Never heard of him. So what?'

'He could be the next sheriff of this town.'

'You don't say! Judge Tarrant could also hold an election and allow the folks of this town to have a say.'

'Ain't likely,' sneered Otto Tribe.

'Wal, now who in hell are you to voice an opinion?'

Otto Tribe hunched forward ominously in his saddle. 'And who the goddam hell are you, cheapskate?'

Bertram Wast smiled thinly and held up a gloved hand. 'Don't get so leery, Griffin. I've heard this jigger Trick Grant is a real smart man. Held a sheriff's job out in Arizona. Thought you'd like to know all this, Griffin. You figure to stay on as Deputy?'

'Maybe. And maybe I'll get the folks of Greenlands to vote in a sheriff. I'll be a candidate an' if they vote for me at least they'll know what they are getting.'

Wast glared. 'Do you figure that to be a smart play? Thought I heard you were looking around to set yourself up on your own spread?'

'Plenty o' time.'

Wast nodded slowly. 'Guess it's a question of holdin' a conference with Judge Tarrant when he arrives this afternoon.'

'You seem to be mighty interested in the choice of a sheriff, Wast?'

Jack saw the man's poker face settle again. 'Naturally I'm interested. As a leading citizen of this town, I know there can't be progress and trade without law an' order. I'm interested in law and order, Griffin.'

Jack decided on a verbal onslaught. 'Then you might be kinda tickled pink to learn that three of your hands tried to shoot Ern Spiceland off his ranch yesterday afternoon. I had to plug one – in self-defence of course. Name of Jed Slacks. He's dead – but I guess you might know that. Some galoot took the body right out of this office last night. Now I figure that's not law an' order, Mister Wast.'

Jack saw Otto Tribe and Red Holbin stiffen in their saddles. Both men shot oblique glances out of narrowed eyes at their boss.

'Ted Slacks doesn't work for me, Griffin. I fired him two days ago. Sure interested to hear your tale, though. I figured he was bad – not my kind of hand. Can't figure why he should be shooting around the Round-O place.'

Jack saw it was useless to expect the rancher to reveal any useful clues that could be used against him. With a thin smile on his lips, Jack began to make himself a cigarette, wondering why he bothered himself with a dirty Indian habit.

Bertram Wast and his men jigged their horses forward. 'Adios, deputy! Just thought you might be interested to hear about Judge Tarrant.'

There were derisory laughs from the other men and then they moved away, their sleek horses headed for the Red Pine Saloon further down the main drag. There were private rooms where a man like Wast could talk and plan without being overheard.

Jack spent some time in another saloon where some waddies from an outlying were making free with the strong drink. He asked questions, mainly about Mike Capstaff. He was hoping some man had a clue about the outlaw out in the Panhandle trails or maybe some cowboy had cut the man's sign. But news about the bad man seemed to have dried up. Or maybe no one was talking.

If he could get a lead on the owl-hoot, it might be possible to collect a posse and ride out. Or alternatively he could go after the man himself.

But there was no information to gather, not even the slightest wild clue. Jack went back to his office, dissatisfied.

He was out in the street to meet the afternoon stage when it rattled in from Abilene. Judge Tarrant was among a few passengers. He was an elderly man in black city clothes. He had a grey head and a stern expression that hardly seemed to alter. Maybe he couldn't smile. Maybe he had forgotten how.

Quite a party gathered in the sheriff's office. There was Jack Griffin, watching with keen interest, Judge

Tarrant and Trick Grant, the man he had brought along. Bertram Wast was present with an adopted air of interest becoming to a leading citizen. Doc Turner and Al Bride, as important men of the town, were there, too. They had been along to see the stage and, interested, had gone along to the office.

Trick Grant was a tall road guy with gunman stamped into his every movement, from his glinting eyes to his clean supple hands. He was dark-haired with some grey. His face was coarse and tough as leather. If he had been a sheriff somewhere else, the town had evidently been full of lawlessness. At least that was Jack's immediate thoughts. He looked again at the man's hands. They were not the fingers of a range waddy. The guy had not done a hard day's graft for a long time.

Judge Tarrant was accustomed to speaking with authority and he began to address the meeting.

'Gentlemen, we are aware of the unfortunate death of Sheriff Tom Mortimer. The murderer will be brought to justice. And for that event, Greenlands as a thriving township needs a new sheriff. As you know I have the power invested in me as a senior judge of Abilene County to swear in a new sheriff. I propose, therefore, to appoint Mr Ted Grant, better known as Trick, to the office of lawman. Can we agree on that, gentlemen?'

Before anyone could utter a word in approval or protest, Jack Griffin snapped out. 'I'm against it!'

'Yeah?' This from Bertram Wast.

'I want a vote from the people. It's their town, ain't it?'

'Huh – bastard! So that's him!' This from Trick Grant, his voice full of insolence.

'I think we should go to the people and ask them

who they want for a sheriff.'

'You figure to stand, huh?' Trick Grant infused hostility into his remark. Evidently he itched to oppose Jack Griffin.

'Yeah, I aim to be sheriff.' Jack watched all the various expressions.

There was a dead silence. Trick Grant had his fingers near his gun, evidently his usual reaction to opposition but of course there were too many men present for him to take action. Judge Tarrant looked a bit nonplussed. His eyes sought those of Bertram Wast as if seeking advice. Jack intercepted the glance and began thinking rapidly.

'If anyone objects to the proposed appointment of Mr Grant, then he can legally claim an election,' said Judge Tarrant very slowly. 'But it's simpler to allow me to appoint a man.'

'I second that,' snapped Wast.

'It isn't a proposal,' put in Doc Turner.

'Aw, hell, who do these guys think they are!' growled Trick Grant.

'I'm the hombre who's objecting to the suggestion that Mister Grant be made sheriff,' said Jack firmly. 'I figure an election is a fair way of settlin' the matter. I admit I have a hankering to be made sheriff. At the moment I'm holding the job of deputy. It ain't enough. If I was the sheriff I'd need a deputy and I could swear him in. That's the usual way.'

Doc Turner nodded. 'That's so. It's all the same to me. I don't keep law. I just patch 'em up. What do you say, Al Bride?'

'Sure. Let's have a Greenlands man elected.'

'You are wasting your time, Griffin.' The snarl of displeasure came from Wast. 'You are wasting your time – and ours. Maybe the folks of this town won't want you.'

'Maybe.' Jack turned, smiling. 'But we could try, huh? Maybe I'd make a better job of it.'

There was an air of reluctance about Judge Tarrant. For a man who was used to making decisions, he seemed momentarily stumped. And once again Jack noticed him glance quickly at Bertram Wast.

It was Doc Turner who made them act. 'Wal, if we are going to have an election, let's get going. Always plenty of fun at an election. Some folks get drunk an' some folks get shot!'

'Sure,' said Al Bride. 'We can hold an election in no time. Joe Blade's got a printing press that can knock off enough voting slips in a few hours. Marvellous machine. Joe says some day they'll be able to print newspapers in an hour.'

'Shit!' muttered Trick Grant. 'By hell, give me that lawman's badge an' I'll soon sort out this load of crap!'

'You'd better start thinking out some speeches, Jack!' laughed Al Bride.

Bertram Wast seemed to make up his mind. 'All right. Mister Grant here will put up for sheriff in opposition, naturally.'

'Why naturally?' asked Jack.

'Because there are important men in Greenlands who don't like you. You'll find that out.'

Jack figured that sounded like a threat. But with the decision, the men stamped out of the office and went different ways. Bertram Wast went off with Judge Tarrant, Jack noticed with a grim smile. The way he was beginning to figure it, Wast must be pretty clever to be able to influence an Abilene judge.

Obviously Wast wanted Trick Grant as sheriff. And just as obvious, Trick Grant had orders, and not only understood them but was prepared to carry them out to the limit. His weight of guns proved that. Or was he all bullying show? Maybe it would be a good idea to find out something about this arrogant man's past.

Doc Turner and Al Bride as dutiful citizens of Greenlands went off to set the election in progress. It would be a simple affair. There would be a few hours' delay while the slips were being printed on the slow hand-press and then the election would soon begin. In a rough and ready way, but with justice, the votes would be counted and the result made known that night.

Jack went to the livery and saddled his roan, spent some time giving the animal a gentle rub down and talking gently into its ear. A horse was a living thing and not just something to be run into the ground. He had decided to ride to the Round-O and inform Ern and Bandy Manners about the election. With a swift ride, he just had time to make the journey.

He fed spurs to the animal as the sun began to climb. Soon the terrain would be really warm. He kept to the defined trail which led out of town and over the flat Panhandle. Over on the horizon was the blur of the foothills which marked Ern's spread. Soon he was a solitary figure crossing the mesquite and shale. This land, he thought, was so huge there was no end to it and why men should fight for vast chunks of it was difficult to understand. But greedy men like Wast wanted more.

He was crouched low on the roan when a shot rang out from the nearby butte. He heard the whistle of the slug over his head and knew it for steel-jacketed rifle shell.

Why it did not knock him from his saddle he did not know. The gun-man had maybe been in a hurry.

Sure as hell it wasn't a warning shot. The bullet had hissed inches from him.

Jack pulled his rifle from the saddle boot and with the same swift motion flung himself from the horse. This action took mere seconds. And even as he leaped from his running cayuse, another shell screamed over the roan's back.

Had he been in the saddle, the bullet would have sliced into his guts. The dirty marksman had the range now.

Jack went staggering forward under the impetus of his own movement. The fine roan, scared by the sudden shots, pranced away in a swift circle and then slowed, turning a head towards Jack.

Jack went on and with a rush slithered into cover behind a large boulder. He lay still for a moment, sizing up his position. The large butte lay ahead, concealing the hidden bushwhacker. All around him was brush, mostly catsclaw and mesquite, with shale and clumps of tough bunch grass. Ahead were the foothills that led to the small canyons and buttes. All this poor-quality land skirted Ern's boundaries. Ern would have a hard job to keep the brush at bay.

The attacker was silent. Hidden somewhere, a guy who had played this mean trick before in his life. Jack decided to try him out.

He used the old trick of raising his hat on the edge of his rifle. The concealed bushwhacker fell for the trick. A bullet screamed across the silent land and maybe scared a distant buzzard. Jack kept well down. Well, at least he knew the galoot had not ridden away.

He knew he had to take a risk if he wanted to pin-point the attacker. He had to look out, draw the man's fire and return it. Maybe he'd get lucky. Maybe. There was also always the chance he'd get a slug in his head.

On his very first peep out he saw a rifle poke from a large rock at the base of the butte. He ducked back as a shot rang out and whined into the boulder and spat dust and chips into his face.

Okay, so the man was a fair shot! It was a grim situation. Now who the hell was trying to kill him? Hell, some jasper had seen him ride out of Greenlands, surely. Maybe. Well, the guy wanted him dead for sure. One of Wast's paid men? Must be! This was lonely land and men did not just hang around waiting for someone to kill.

The rock was quite hot. This stalemate could go on for hours unless the bushwhacker simply rode away. The swine had large cover, more than a damned boulder. He also had a horse hidden somewhere, probably near a crevice in the butte.

Jack glanced sideways and noticed the shallow depression just a few yards away. It ran like a shallow crack in the ground for a fair distance and it curved around closer to the butte where the attacker must be. But the amount of cover it afforded was frighteningly poor.

All the same he determined to try for the slit. It seemed the only way he could get near to this unknown bushwhacker. Of course, he had his rifle and a Colt for short distances.

He wished he could get rid of the killer instinct but it had served him in the past and maybe this wasn't the right time for these philosophies. He had to kill this rat or be killed!

Tensed, he sprang like coiled steel. He streaked like a mountain cat for the shallow draw. The bushwhacker got busy at his first sighting and deadly shots spattered the ground, all rifle bullets. Slugs spat into the earth, digging deep. Well, it wasn't his flesh the bullets were finding, thank God! Seconds later he flung himself flat into the shallow crack in the earth, safe for the moment!

He stayed only a few minutes, feeling that he had only that amount of time. He snaked forward on all fours with real speed, keeping to the bottom of the earth-crack like a snake.

Even so, owing to the undulating nature of the ground, he evidently afforded momentary glimpses of himself to the man behind the butte, for, as he moved along the slit, slugs followed him viciously. But every one was a miss. The man was just frantically snapping off shots.

The swine had to reload; time for Jack to move quickly. He went along the shale bottom of the slit with his head scraping the ground. He hoped there weren't any rattlers sunning in the slit. And there was another thought. He hoped his attacker would not climb to the top of the butte. Because that way the man could get a bead on his victim in the shallow, twisting trench.

And then after some moments of desperate slithering forward, Jack reached the end of the strange slit in the earth. The ground levelled out. Only clumps of scrub were around him, hardly providing real cover. He had only to lift his head and the bushwhacker would have a prime target.

Jack knew he had to move again, but real fast. The attacker would guess he was at the limit of the shallow draw and would have his rifle trained on the spot.

The mass of the butte was real close, of course, rising from the bed of the land hardly twenty yards away. The bushwhacker was hidden on the left side of the rocky outcrop. The swine was evidently a sticker.

But maybe he just figured he had a good chance of killing his victim.

It was a tough situation he had gotten himself into. But if he had continued his ride on the roan, the attacker out there would have got him with the second or third bullet.

Jack moved his rifle up, held it with two hands against his hip. Tensed, he knew he had to get up against that butte. He had to move.

There was a brooding silence all around him, the vast land simply silent, the sun high and now brassy. There were no cattle or riders around this area. Nothing stirred – unless there was an unseen rattler somewhere in the rocks. He was just a guy hugging the earth for protection, a primitive feeling that would come over any fugitive creature. Ahead of him, hidden, was an unknown enemy. Strangely, he was beginning to wonder just what kind of bastard wanted him dead.

It was grim and unpleasant to slap up against the stark fact that you did not know if you would emerge dead or alive from the next few minutes. It was not the first time in his life that he had felt this way. He remembered the time he had to kill the Mex – but he did not want to reflect on that nasty moment.

He might spill his life blood on the arid land, or it might be the other hombre. Seemingly, they were playing for keeps. Who was this grim rannigan? Maybe a hired hand.

Jack Griffin did not want to die like this. In fact, he really had no wish to kill again. A man never forgot the guy he had killed.

Suddenly, furious with everything, he sprang out, as fast as the bullets that began to spit at him. Even as he jumped into the open, his own rifle began to bark.

He ran, leaped and hugged the weapon close to his hip, firing all the time.

Crack! Crack! He could feel the gun was alive! Like himself it was fighting back!

He sent the shots against the edge of the butte. This had the immediate effect of stopping the other man's fire. Probably the guy had dived for cover. Jack could not aim accurately as he ran, but he emptied the rifle at the spot ahead.

As he moved, his boots dug desperately at the shale and grass tufts, impelling himself on and on. His long legs leaped for the wall of the butte, his heart beating fast, and he made the cover just as his gun clicked. Empty!

Then he was flat against the rocky surface of the towering butte and there was comfort in the mass of rock. He marvelled that the bushwhacker's first bullet had not found him during that critical running leap. His own rataplan of fire had deterred the man. Jack knew the man was somewhere in the cover of the irregular rocky butte. The guy was waiting for him to make a false move.

Well, the hell with him! He silently reloaded his rifle with the shells he had in a pocket. Inside him was this savage feeling that he had to press on. One had to die!

He was as tightly strung as a mountain lion stalking its prey. His mouth was a thin taut line. His eyes were narrowed. The killer instinct did not make for a pretty sight. His wits were racing around the problem of how to get the grim bastard.

Damn the man! What was he risking his life for? Was he so confident in his killing ability to take these chances for money?

Jack was grimly pleased that he was now on equal

terms with his would-be killer. He was no longer a man hugging the earth and praying, and pray he had, hit with the knowledge he had a lot to live for.

Confident, he shouted: 'I'm a-comin' to get yuh, hombre!'

He waited, hardly breathing. There was deep silence, hanging low over the terrain like a tangible thing. Nothing moved. He might have been a crazy man talking to the rocky silent butte. Then a voice thick with anger came back at him.

'You talk too much, Griffin. Don't over-play your hand.'

Jack thought he recognised the voice, the deep vocal tones. His eyes narrowed as he concentrated. The words had carried savage hate, he realised, but maybe it was just the fury of a man who had been outsmarted. Jack figured to compel the guy to talk again, thinking he might get another clue. 'Maybe you'll tell me what you got against me, stranger?'

'Maybe! You can go to hell figuring it out for yourself!'

Jack did not give the man the satisfaction of an answer for two reasons. One, he had identified the man. He was sure he was dealing with Red Holbin who, only that morning, had gone into town with Bertram Wast. He had heard that unpleasant voice many times before in the saloons. Second, Jack did not intend to speak again because he realised he might be giving away his position. At first he had spoken in the exultation of the moment. Now he was more wary. He had even figured out Red Holbin's position from the sound of his voice. The man was no more than twenty yards away, around the jagged curve of the rocky wall.

Swiftly, he realised that the man who got to the top

of the butte first would have the drop on his enemy. He could look down over the edge or manoeuvre until he had his opponent at his mercy. The man below would have little cover.

Jack reached up for hand-holds. He hitched his leg up and began to climb, making no sounds at that moment. He couldn't be sure to keep as silent as that for very long. He slung his rifle over his back, adjusted his hat and reached up lithely. He hauled himself up another two yards. This was a task that needed agility and here he knew he had the advantage over Red Holbin. The man was older than himself and he liked cigars and drank too much in the saloons. He was pretty sure that the murderous guy could not climb the butte wall without making a lot of noise and giving himself away.

Jack did not stop once to listen. There was the same silence all around the brooding place. He hauled himself up another yard or so without noise. Even an Indian could not have bettered his onward movement. He went on, making sure his rifle did not touch rock. Ah, another yard, with difficult handholds and root-holds. He was nearing the top.

He was a little shocked at his grim intention to kill this man. But Red Holbin, under orders, had set the challenge. The old law of the wild stabbed through his brain. Kill or be killed! The elemental gut feeling was a lousy thing to entertain but that was the way this play had gone.

Jack slowly hauled himself on to the loose surface of the flat-topped butte, sending chippings sliding down to the bottom. Red Holbin would surely hear these sounds.

There was brush growing on this small plateau. He went on, crouching, taking care not to dislodge more loose shale. The butte was about thirty feet in height, a mass of rock left by some freak of nature as the land all around sank or eroded over the centuries.

Then suddenly he was at the edge of the rock and his first glimpse of his enemy was somehow strange. The man was below, flat against the rock, behind a small abutment that would give him cover from any approaching man on his level. He obviously did not suspect that Jack was above him. Red Holbin had Colts withdrawn. He was listening, his whole body ready for trigger-work. He was a killer waiting for the other man to make a move. Then his guns would blaze lead, gambling on sheer speed to win the fight.

The loose shale had not warned him.

For a few seconds Jack stood still, his gut hard and tense, trying hard to hate this man. It wasn't always easy to hate. He was an enemy who wanted to kill him. Red Holbin would have laughed as guts spilled in blood and flesh – as long as it wasn't his own. The man wanted to stalk like the predator he was, so he would have to take his chance all the way to hell.

'Red Holbin,' Jack called out softly.

He had to warn the guy, in a voice devoid of expression. Jack Griffin could not kill in cold blood.

Red Holbin jerked. His guns flew upwards. His face contorted with sudden fear as he realised he was at risk, taken by surprise.

Jack Griffin shot from the waist with his rifle before the other man's guns steadied, triggering once, twice, three times in rapid fire. The first bullet hacked into Red Holbin and he staggered back. Despite his movement, the other shots found the target as Jack Griffin aimed instinctively.

Red Holbin lurched back against the rock face as the slugs found their soft target. He fell back, sliding down slowly, with an incredulous expression on his twitching, ugly face. His guns dropped from nerveless hands. He went down like a sack, blood gushing from his mouth. A hole near his heart spurted redness as he died.

Jack climbed down from his position and heard the neigh of a horse in fright and he knew Red Holbin had been waiting for him ready to hand out death. Well, the man got his come-uppance!

The ambusher's horse was ground-hitched in the cover of the butte wall. Well, he sure would not need that nag any more. What he needed was a burial party.

The answer to the attempted bushwhack was pretty obvious. The man had been ordered to kill because someone did not want Jack Griffin as sheriff of Greenlands. There was no other reason.

And Jack could guess easily enough that Bertram Wast was the man who did not want him to be sheriff. Wast had sent a hired gun-hand to kill. It seemed that Wast had figured that was the only way he could be sure Jack did not win the election. Dead men could not stand for the office of sheriff.

Now why was Bertram Wast so intent upon having Trick Grant as sheriff of Greenlands? Well, they were thick as thieves but probably there were many other reasons.

4

Enter Ezra Hide

Jack Griffin worked quickly to bury Red Holbin. It was a simple matter to heap rocks and shale over the lifeless body. He took the man's guns. Maybe he might have to prove that the guy was dead and the guns would be sufficient. He had no intention of taking the cadaver back to town. He was content to know he had won the grim fight. Red Holbin had been defeated by gunsmoke justice. Along with Jed Slacks, he was the second of Wast's hands to go.

Obviously, it had been known that Jack had ridden out of town. Wast had sent his trusted killer to ride quickly and get ahead to a spot where he could shoot at the man who wanted to be sheriff of Greenlands.

With the body covered, Jack stamped off for his horse. The animal had calmed down and was nosing for grass. As for Red Holbin's crittur, Jack figured the animal would return to the Bar-K in its own time. Wast would know the answer to his trickery when the horse returned riderless.

The more he thought about the ruthless attempt to get rid of him, the more he was determined to stand for the office of sheriff. His plan to settle on a ranch of his own could wait a little longer until he got to the end of this crooked play by Wast.

He rowelled the roan in order to make fast speed to Ern's ranch. Soon the trail skirted the broken country. An hour later he rode a tired animal into the Round-O ranch yard and leaped to the ground.

Ern Spiceland was in the yard, mending the pole corral. Fred and Jane were there, taking time off from the ranch chores. They all glanced swiftly at Jack. He walked up stiffly. Jane took the leathers of his horse. It was Ern who realised there was something amiss. His sharp eyes searched Jack's dust-coated face.

'Thought you'd like to know there's goin' to be an election in town,' said Jack. 'Judge Tarrant came in from Abilene with a hombre called Trick Grant who was all set to just take over, with the help of certain friends, but I've claimed an election. Not that that makes me popular with Wast.'

And then he told them about Red Holbin. Jane seemed fearful as he briefy outlined the events. 'He could have killed you!'

Jack grinned. 'But he didn't.'

'You've got yourself in bad with Wast now,' observed Ern. 'Can you figure any reason why he wants Trick Grant as sheriff?'

Jack rolled a cigarette deftly, feeling some need for the weed. 'Nope! Can't rightly say why Wast seems keen to get that Grant hombre installed. But I've a hunch he's planned it all long ago. He is mighty pally with Judge Tarrant. Too pally.'

'And I believe that Wast is behind the death of Tom Mortimer and his deputy,' said Jane indignantly.

'You see, proof has to be obtained for all these things to be taken seriously,' muttered Jack Griffin. 'And it was Mike Capstaff who shot Tom Mortimer and Sam Brant.'

'That may be so,' she said firmly. 'But I feel Bertram Wast is at the bottom of it. This is a woman's intuition. I don't like Wast.'

Jack and Ern grinned suddenly.

'I kinda agree, Jane,' Ern nodded. 'But you can't pin things on a galoot just because you don't like him!'

Jane tossed her head angrily. 'He's a scoundrel!'

'All we've got are a lot of hunches,' said Jack. 'They're mighty interestin' an' I got plenty myself. But I need something definite to pin on Bertram Wast. It's still all kinda vague. Did you get them cows hidden away, Ern?'

'Sure. Bandy is out right now, ridin' the spread to see if any hombres come this way.'

Jack smiled slightly. 'It looks mighty like if Bertram Wast is waitin' until he's got a sheriff he likes in that office before he comes looking for his cattle. Suppose he had Trick Grant with him and he finds those longhorns with the worked-over brands? Why, then, they might even put you on the end of a hangnoose and answer questions afterwards, Ern!'

'What an awful thing to say!' Jane looked alarmed.

Jack and Ern laughed. 'He ain't finding them,' said Ern. 'Bandy and me have got them hidden pretty good. Them beeves are right back in the foothills now. It would take weeks of searching around to find 'em unless they were powerful lucky.'

'That's fine. You coming to town to vote? I've got to get back an' waste no time. I guess I've got to speak to the folks of Greenlands. They expect me to say somethin'. Sure don't know what to say exactly.'

And Jack rubbed the back of his head as if confronted with a problem.

'Just tell the people you stand for law and justice for rich and poor alike,' said Jane quickly.

He saw the gleam in her clear eyes. He looked steadily into them and saw the flush mount in her cheeks. She was bronzed, lovely, a desirable woman and suddenly he realised he was a fool if he didn't do something quickly about these feelings. There were other guys who might beat him to this wonderful girl.

'I'll remember that,' he said. He repeated the words. 'Law and justice for rich and poor alike.' He nodded, grinned. 'That's just the words I wanted. Thanks, Jane.'

He did not know the way she felt, but she thrilled at his sincere compliment.

'I'll ride in with you,' decided Ern Spiceland. 'I got a right to vote. Bandy will be coming back pretty soon for chow. Tell him where I am, Fred. I figure you should get back to the hotel, Jane.'

'I'll stay here and help Bandy. I'm too young to vote,' said Fred.

'And I'm a woman,' Jane said angrily, 'and I haven't the right to vote in that man's town! And that's something that should be changed, Jack Griffin!'

He laughed and turned away. 'You'll be all right at the Packhorse.'

'The way you talk you'd think I couldn't take care of myself!' With a laugh she flashed the remark back at him.

'Remember Greenlands is a lawless burg in some ways.' Jack grinned at her. 'But as long as I'm around you can call on me if anyone makes trouble for you, Jane.'

Once again their eyes met. He wished he could invent smart flattery, the way some men did with women, but glib words stuck in his throat.

Fred Spiceland stayed at the ranch so there was contact with Bandy when he got back. Some minutes later the three rode out at a smart pace on refreshed horses and hit the trail for town. They covered the undulating varied landscape at a fair lick and eventually came into the busy cowtown. With animals covered with dust and lather, Jack and the other two took the horses straight to the livery near the Packhorse Hotel and gave instructions to water, rub down and feed the mounts.

Jane went into the hotel to change into more feminine attire. She had been wearing blue jeans and a shirt which was distinctly mannish. Greenlands, striving hard to achieve some degree of civilisation like the distant town of Abilene, frowned on ladies who moved around its streets looking like slim youths.

Jack and Ern went along to Joe Blade's one-man printing works to see what progress had been made with the voting slips. Doc Turner and Al Bride were busybodying around. It was the usual kind of excitement that preceded an election, and if the issue were not so serious, Jack might have found plenty to laugh at.

There were calls for him to make a speech. reluctantly, Jack climbed on to the verandah of the printing office and hammered on the rail with his Colt butt for some sort of silence.

'Folks, I'm not saying much.' A small number of people had gathered. 'You know that a town which is growing fast like Greenlands must have law and order – for everyone's sake. And for that you need a good sheriff. Maybe I'm that kind of man. It's up to the folks to decide. You also know that Tom Mortimer and Sam Brant were killed by an outlaw name o' Mike Capstaff. If I'm elected sheriff, I promise to get that no-good hombre even if it takes a long time to trail and hog-tie him. He'll get a fair trial, unless he figures to shoot it out first – an' then he'll get a fair burial. I promise you law and justice for rich an' poor alike. That's all, folks.'

He was about to step down when he saw Bertram Wast ride up on a big horse and halt on the edge of the crowd, looking an imposing figure in a black suit and hat with a wide brim. The rancher sat his saddle and stared grimly at Jack Griffin and then spoke in grating tones.

'I'll take you up on that, feller. I figure Ern Spiceland has got cattle of mine on his land – and don't tell me they're strays. I've been losing stock lately – so my foreman tells me. I want an investigation. As deputy, you went out to get Ern Spiceland under Tom Mortimer's instructions but he conveniently got away from you. Now I see you two galoots are mighty pally. Can I ask what you are going to do about this rustling?'

Jack could guess that Wast was raging inside at Red Holbin's failure to eliminate him.

'I've been to the Round-O and looked around,' Jack retorted. 'I can't find any evidence of rustling. There's nothing but Round-O stock on that spread.'

He knew that Wast was aware that he was lying, for the man knew that the over-branded cows were on the Round-O range.

Jack enjoyed the undercurrent of hostility. The more that was said, the more he could guess at Wast's motives. What was the man's game? What was his play? Why did he want Ern's ranch?

Jack knew instantly that Wast was trying to stir up trouble. There were many ranchers and cowboys in town that day and they hated rustling more than any other crime.

'I figure you're not so good as a lawman, Griffin,' snarled Wast, his temper flaring. 'If you can't locate a few rustled steers, I challenge your capacity to deal with the problems of this town as sheriff. I want to tell the folks of Greenlands that I support Trick Grant. This man has a fine record. If he is elected as sheriff, I'll get him to deal with the missing stock. And if the people of this town are so misguided as to elect you as sheriff, Griffin, I'll take my men to the Round-O range and deal with this rustling myself as soon as I find evidence.'

'Better not over-play your hand, Wast,' snapped Jack.

The rancher wheeled his horse and jigged it down the main street. A hubbub arose among the crowd of cowhands, store-keepers, cattlemen and others who had listened to the exchange of words.

The crowd slowly dispersed. Not all took the proposed election very seriously, especially the kind of men who had scant regard for the law in any case. The actual voting was due to start at about four o'clock. With a small population of real voters, the verdict would be known very quickly and the affair discussed perhaps in the saloons and stores and wherever people gathered.

Jack felt pretty confident of his chances. He was known to the folks of Greenlands and Trick Grant was really an unknown factor. Wast must be aware of this disturbing fact. Apparently he had thought Jack would step down when Judge Tarrant had brought the man along. Or maybe he had counted on a successful outcome to the attempted bushwhack?

The thing that bothered Jack Griffin were the possible motives Wast had for his crooked play. Why did he try to plant Bar-K cattle on Ern's spread? If it was because he wanted to crowd Ern off his ranch, why in heck did he need that poor land?

Bertram Wast had arrived in the Greenlands area five years ago. It was soon apparent the man was out for power. He had arrived as a stranger and during a drought year began buying land. He seemed to have the resources, either in cash or with a placket of tricks no other man would pull. He had taken up leases, filed claims on free range. Soon he was a big guy in that territory. Why should he try to obtain the Round-O by fair means or foul?

Jack had to admit he had been away a long time from bounty-hunting. Looking back he knew that had been a grim time.

During the years Wast had gained in power and presumably wealth. And now he wanted Ern's range. Surely the guy didn't really need it? Was Wast just a grasping bastard? Or was there another reason? His waddies had tried to burn the ranch-house; the cattle were planted on Ern's land. And there was the question over the body of Jed Slacks which had mysteriously disappeared from the sheriff's office. Then Red Holbin – Wast's man without a doubt – had tried his hand at a murderous bushwhack. It all added up – but to what?

Then how did the murders of Tom Mortimer and Sam Brant add into this score? Who had paid Mike Capstaff to murder? And for what reason?

'Guess I'll discover the answers sooner or later,' muttered Jack. 'And even if I'm voted out I'll work on finding Mike Capstaff on a free-lance basis. Tom was a good feller, although I figger now he knew Wast's accusations were faked.'

Jack went along to the saloon with Ern. He was not a hard drinker but he liked the conviviality of the saloon men. Right now he felt he needed a drink.

'That snakeroo aims to stir up trouble for me,' Ern confided. 'All that talk about rustling won't do me much good in this cow-town. I oughta go for him with a six-shooter!'

'Don't try. Maybe that's what he wants. He's got gun-hands around him. He doesn't carry a weapon. He's an eastern hombre.'

The voting began a bit later and for the next few hours Jack felt strangely restless. Jane and he stood on the boardwalk of the Packhorse Hotel and watched the crowds drift past. It was noticeable that many Bar-K hands were in town. In fact, the whole outfit seemed to be on hand. And they would have their orders.

At the ballot boxes Doc Turner, Al Bride, Joe Blade and a few more reputable men of the area were stationed. It was a rough and ready election but it would be fair so far as anyone could see.

Jack did not intend to reveal he had killed Red Holbin in a fair fight. He would leave it to Wast to start anything.

It was hours later when the result of the Greenlands election was known. The result was overwhelmingly in favour of Jack Griffin, a clear majority. It only remained for him to be sworn in by Judge Tarrant, a formality that seemed to be taken for granted. Whether the judge would relish the task was dubious.

The swearing-in was done with curt ceremony inside the sheriff's office. Tarrant's expression was unpleasant. He had been outsmarted, an experience not to his liking.

Jack turned to Ern Spiceland. 'How about you being deputy?'

'I got my ranch to attend to.'

'Sure. Plenty of deputies have ranches or jobs. It ain't a full-time job.'

A gleam appeared in Ern's bright eyes. 'Hell, why not? Has any jasper present got any objections?'

Judge Tarrant shook his head, dispensing with speech. Doc Turner was present but Bertram Wast, evidently raging at the election verdict, was absent.

'It don't matter about objections,' said Jack. 'As sheriff I can swear you in as my deputy. That's the way it is in any town.'

And in a rough and ready manner they went ahead with the oath. It was a brisk proceeding conducted by men who knew the taking of a lawman's job was often a ticket to Boothill or at the least a parcel of grief.

Jack pinned a deputy badge on Ern's flapping vest. He wore a sheriff's star on his own gaberdine check shirt.

'All right, you can get back to your spread, Ern, but sooner or later we'll have work to do with some desperado.'

'Suits me. But let me buy you a drink. Remember, I owe you somethin' for that crack on the head I gave you!'

They spent some time in the saloon and various rannigans congratulated Jack. Mostly the men were decent hard-working trail hands, but a few of the Bar-K were in the drinking place and their hard glances were an indication of where their loyalties lay. One guy jostled Jack Griffin and breathed smelly breath right into his face.

'Heh, heh, Mister sheriff! Cain't say I like lawmen – especially the jumped-up kind!'

'Do you figure to spend the rest of the day in a cell?' Jack called the man's bluff. The man waved a dirty hand and ambled off, boozed to the eyes.

Ern set off for his distant spread and Jack rode out with him some way and then had to leave his deputy. Jack came back to his office and spent some time making out a reward notice. He intended to offer some of his hard-earned money as a reward for Mike Capstaff, dead or alive.

He was sitting at the rough desk before the empty cells thinking they would look fine if only one or two were filled with Wast's rannigans, when a knock sounded on the outer door.

Jack got up, hand near a gun-butt, and opened the door to admit a dirty, whiskered man of indeterminate age. 'Yeah? What can I do for you? I don't know you.'

'You want to locate Mike Capstaff?' Old beady eyes gleamed at the new sheriff.

'Sure, but I hope you ain't foolin'.'

'Not me,' mumbled the man. 'I jest got into town – heerd all this rumpus about a new sheriff. I heard about Mike Capstaff killin' Tom Mortimer. Mighty fine gent was Tom – friend o' mine, yeah. I've been up in the hills, lookin' fer gold an' I don't know much about the goings-on in town but –'

'Get to the point, old-timer.'

'Yeah, sure will. Like I say, I been looking fer gold. I know all the durned folk around here say there ain't no gold but they's too iggerant to know better.'

'Have you got something to tell me?' Jack grinned.

'Sure. You in some sort of hurry, huh? Ain't you interested in gold? Huh? There's plenty but I never struck a bonanza.'

'You said something about Mike Capstaff.'

'Yeah. I cut his sign when I was up in them hills beyond the Panhandle. That's all. I seen him. He made a camp in a cave in that twisted canyon – a rocky hideout. I watched him 'cause I knowed him for a bad hombre. I figure he's living up there. Maybe he hunts his grub – plenty of small animals up there. I just came away quiet-like. Seems a loner – didn't like the look of his guns – so I crept away. Never thought much more about him until I hit town and then I heard about Tom being gunned down.'

'What makes you think this galoot was Mike Capstaff?'

'I knowed him!' shouted the old-timer.

'Good. Can you lead me to that canyon?'

'Sure can but I need a drink. It's mighty hard on a jigger to hit town after being up in them hills for weeks and then have to leave town again.'

'What do you want? Money?'

Ezra's eyes gleamed. 'Nope. I need a drink. A good drink. Dust in them hills gets in a man's throat pretty bad.'

Jack grabbed his arm, fingers clawing through the dirty, old deerskin jacket. 'What about showing me the way up to that cave where you spotted Capstaff – tonight!'

'Tonight! Hell, I'm plumb tired! An' what about my drink?'

'I'll buy you a bottle of General Grant right now and you can sup while you ride, huh? And you ain't tired – not an ornery feller like you!'

'Me! Tired! Me – Ezra Hide! Hell! Even a young jigger like you couldn't tire me!'

'You just said you were tired.'

'Hell – you tryin' to rile me? I meant I was tired of bein' without a damned drink!'

'Are you loco?'

'Me! Nope! Hell, you are trying to rile me, mister.'

Jack reached for his hat and rifle. 'You got a hoss?'
'Nope.'
'What in heck have you got?'
'I take a mule along with me into them hills.'

'We'll get along faster with you on a horse,' said Jack. 'I'll get you a fresh animal. Come along with me. I'll get you a horse and a bottle. How far do you reckon it is to the cave in the canyon?'

'Maybe forty miles. Maybe less. If you're settin' off now, reckon it'll take all night to ride.'

'Reckon so,' agreed Jack. 'And it's pretty hard country once we get out of the limit of the flat Panhandle. I'll need a fresh cayuse, too. Reckon I'd better rest the roan.'

He took the dirty, bewhiskered old-timer along to the livery stable and got the animals. He had to roust out the stableman from the comfort of his cabin at the rear of the livery. Jack led out a handsome steeldust gelding for himself and a bay sorrel for Ezra, a more than adequate animal for the old-timer. As Ezra had no saddle except the worn gear on his mule, a saddle rig had to be obtained from the livery man. Jack led the horses along to his office and rigged his saddle on the steeldust gelding. He stuffed some grub into a saddle-bag and tied it on. His ammunition belt was full of slugs for his rifle and Colt.

He was leaving no notice for anyone. He did think of seeing Jane for a minute but it was late. Might be a good notion if little about this ride into the night got around.

Jack got a bottle of whiskey from the office for the old-timer. The guy was broke. He was an old man with a mule and high hopes of finding a bonanza somewhere in the hills. These rumours of gold were often brought into town by drifters. He hoped Ezra wasn't as crazy as his ideas of finding gold might suggest. In a word, he hoped the old prospector's story about Mike Capstaff wasn't another yarn like the one about finding gold in the hills. Somehow, he thought Ezra was speaking the truth.

The two men spaced out their departure from Greenlands. Even at this late hour Jack did not want to be seen, especially as it was obvious at a glance that if they left together it was some sort of expedition.

On the trail outside of town, he caught up with Ezra, a tall erect figure in the saddle. He had donned gloves. He took one off and rolled a cigarette with one hand.

'I'll stick to the bottle,' chuckled Ezra.

After a while they cantered along a fairly even trail with the advantage of a moon. But Jack knew that the combination of night light and rough ground ahead would slow the animals to walking speed.

He had no clear idea about dealing with the outlaw, Mike Capstaff. They might be unlucky and not even catch up with the owlhooter. The man might be moving on, but he'd stick to his trail if it could be found. Ezra Hide had afforded a lead which might be the end of the outlaw. And somewhere along the line Bertram Wast might get his come-uppance.

After two hours of steady canter, they rode the horses into the edge of the broken country, slowing the pace, comforting the edgy animals and giving them time to drink at a convenient shallow pond. Ahead, the hills loomed black and dangerous for night riding.

Ezra seemed to be content with his bottle, raising it frequently to his mouth. He sang a weird old song about a stranger who found a ravine full of gold. Jack grinned thinly, hoping the old-timer would not fall from his horse somewhat the worse for drink.

They rode into butte country well after midnight,

the masses of strangely-shaped rock looking pretty eerie in the wan moonlight. The horses picked a nervous way. From a nearby ridge a coyote suddenly howled. Now and then, from some stand of wood, there was a harsh cry from a night owl. Jack felt tired, events draining him a bit. Ezra seemed to know his way. Loose shale clattered under hoofs and clumps of cactus made the journey difficult.

Towards dawn Ezra threw away the bottle with a cuss. Jack watched him grimly, conscious that he was taking the word of a stranger.

'There's a reward for that hombre, dead or alive, but only when I get him. Are you goin' to ride into his canyon with me?'

'If'n I can git a reward, you bet!'

'Wal, if I've got to draw a gun on him you might only get half the reward,' drawled Jack.

The taunt had no effect on Ezra. 'Now ain't that mighty shrewd of you! I liked Tom Mortimer an' any reward will suit me.'

The sheriff stared around at the shadowy outcrops of rock. 'That catamount certainly moved himself well out of town.'

'He's only a day's ride from Greenlands.' Ezra cackled shrewdly.

'You're right. And he's hanging around because he figures Wast might need him again.'

There was obviously a good reason why the outlaw was still in the territory. Most outlaws with the murder of two lawmen against them would have moved a long way off. So the murderer was out here in the wild country, hiding, but close enough to get back into town if he was needed. He had not reckoned on an old prospector cutting his sign.

Jack and Ezra rode around the base of the jagged

hill and halted, the canyon before them, shadowy in the half-light. The high walls of the canyon made for deep pools of darkness, changing patterns of semi-light. The canyon bed was almost pure sand, drifting stuff brought in by the winter winds. Jack looked for tracks but could not discern any.

'We'll ground-hitch the horses, then go along on foot. You sure this is the right place?'

'Sure. Twisted canyon, I call it.'

'You can hang back if you like –'

'The hell with you, sheriff. You tryin' to edge me outa my reward?'

'All right. But leave the action to me – if there is any. I want to talk to that hombre. He's more valuable alive than dead.'

Jack drew his Colt and walked ahead, Ezra behind him. He wasn't happy about the oldster being so close. Tackling a killer like Capstaff and nursing an old man was not his idea of fun.

There was a sombre silence in the deep canyon, the walls seeming to suggest a grave. Jack wished the lone coyote would howl. Anything might be better than deadly silence. Surely Capstaff would hear or sense their approach because even the movement of sand breached the brooding silence.

For that reason he stopped every three yards and listened, taut, intent. Ezra was right behind him. Jack wished to hell the man was somewhere else. This was a grim setup, stalking a killer with a crazy old prospector as partner!

There was not a break in the soft night silence that lay like a mantle over the deep canyon. Suddenly Ezra pointed to an abutment of the canyon wall some twenty yards distant. 'That's the cave! Figure he's still there? Mighty quiet, he is. No fire, either!'

Jack nodded, kept his eyes glued on the abutment. He thought he could see a slightly different variation of shadow on the canyon wall. But this pattern was slight. If Mike Capstaff was inside the cave, surely he would have the solace of a fire? The man must be a hard case to endure this mode of existence.

Jack moved step by step, feet pressing so softly into the sand an Indian tracker could not have done better. And even Ezra seemed to have the knack of moving without sound. One clumsy footstep and a man might emerge from the cave with guns flashing flame through the half-light.

Then Jack Griffin smelled the acrid swirl of smoke drifting to him. Wood smoke! A fire was burning somewhere!

Jack turned the edge of the cave mouth and walked in. His boot pressed soft into sand. He went in with his Colt held level and menacing. The next moment he detected the red glow from a damped-down fire at the end of the tunnel-like cave.

A man was there, crouched over the smouldering fire. His back was towards Jack Griffin, a target so tempting. The man was placing bits of dried cactus stalk on the low fire and the thin smoke rose to the high roof of the cave and drifted along to the mouth.

Jack went along another three paces and then hissed. 'Don't move! I'm Jack Griffin, sheriff of Greenlands!'

The bending man froze. Time stood still in a crazy way for all in the cave, even Ezra who had drifted up close.

'You? Sheriff?'

'That's right, Capstaff. And I've got a six-shooter pointed right at you.'

'Mind if I turn around?' The outlaw was cool, sure

thing. 'I'd like to look at the galoot who gets the drop on Mike Captaff!'

'One trick and you're dead!'

There was no sudden response from the outlaw. But his head moved slowly as he tried to look around out the corners of his eyes. He began to breathe harshly as his situation coloured his mind. His hands hung limply, not moving, but almost twitching under the impulse to whip out a gun.

'Get his gun, Ezra.' Jack Griffin never took his gaze off the outlaw. A second's lack of concentration and the man might do something crazy.

'I guess I don't have to tell you, Ezra, not to get across my sights.' The instructions came coolly and the old-timer was wise enough to understand as he plucked the Colt from the leather.

Jack relaxed. The man had a rifle stacked in a corner of the cave, near a saddle and other gear. 'Get that long pole, Ezra.'

The old prospector chuckled delightedly, carefully obeying the instruction. At that moment, Jack was glad of his help.

'I don't have to tell you I'll drill you if you make a move.' The reminder was flung at the outlaw. Then: 'All right, you can turn. But keep your hands up.'

'You got my hog-leg, damn you!'

'Yeah – but you might try to rush me. If you do, you'll die damn quick!'

Mike Capstaff lumbered around. His dark deep eyes stared balefully at the sheriff. He was a big guy in a burly clumsy fashion but there was something about his slight movement that suggested he could whip around swiftly under provocation. His in-bitten nature was stamped across his tight mouth and hard wary eyes. His criminal way of living had etched itself into his mean visage. He was a killer, Jack Griffin had to remind himself.

'What the hell do you want with me?' It was more of a sneer than a sensible question.

'I'm taking you back to town for trial. You killed Tom Mortimer and Sam Brant.'

'They was fair fights.'

'I don't believe that. You're a lying bastard! It was murder.'

'You can go to hell, tin-badge.'

'Wal, I guess I've got to take you back to town for a trial but if I had my way I'd kill you slowly right here and now – a slug in the gut, right low down where your private parts dangle!'

'That's just shit! You ain't the type!' And Mike Capstaff knew he had scored here.' His laugh was thick with insolence.

'I want to hear you talk now,' insisted Jack. 'Who paid you to kill the old sheriff and Sam?'

'I ain't doin' any talking.'

'I can guess your play.' Jack eyed the man grimly. 'You figure Wast might be able to save you somehow when we get you back to town. Maybe I should plug you right now an' save myself some trouble.'

And Jack Griffin raised his Colt with some intent, finger near the trigger, the long barrel pointed at Capstaff's heart.

Fear leaped in the outlaw. 'Don't!'

'You're goin' to talk, pal. I'm not taking you back to town until I've got some information from you. Now why did Wast get you to kill those two lawmen? What is Wast's play? I figure you know.'

'Killin' me won't get you answers you yeller-belly tin-pot sheriff!'

Jack laughed. 'No. But you'll dangle on a rope when

you get back to town.'

'Don't be too sure.'

Mike Capstaff had recovered his confidence somewhat for he hooked his thumb in his belt and laughed with filthy disdain at the sheriff.

'Figure it out, Mister Sheriff. I got friends. Anyway I don't know what the hell you are talking about.'

Jack eyed the burly man grimly. He had weight but Jack felt sure it was soft gut and flabby flesh. He wanted to hurt this guy.

'Ezra,' he called out. 'Put some more brush on that fire. I want more light.'

'You figure to burn him?'

'Nope. Just hurt him and maybe make him talk.'

'Okay, Sheriff – you want more light – you got it.' And Ezra quickly heaped tinder on the low fire. Light illuminated the cave. Shadows danced strangely on the yellow walls of sandstone. Capstaff watched, puzzled but wary, a man of menace – but without guns.

'Ezra, get your gun out an' watch this hombre. You're the referee!'

'Yeah? What in hell d'you aim to do, Sheriff?'

For an answer Jack pushed his gun back in the holster. Capstaff's eyes gleamed at this action. Jack did not take his eyes off the whisker-stubbled face before him and then he began to unbuckle his gun-belt. Soon it dropped to the cave floor and Jack pushed it to a corner with a foot. All the time he was doing this he was sizing up the big man before him.

'You're shit, Capstaff! Soft as muck!'

'You think so? What are you – a blabber-mouth?'

'I'm the sheriff but I'm also a man who likes revenge. Tom Mortimer was a friend o' mine.'

'Mine, too,' cackled Ezra.

Jack raised his fists in the old style of the bare-knuckle fighter. 'You've got a chance, Capstaff. More'n you gave Tom and Sam Brant, I guess.'

Mike Capstaff slowly raised his bunched fists. They looked big and filthy, ominous until Jack glanced at the man's belly.

'I'm goin' to knock hell outa you, Capstaff, until you talk! I want to know who has paid you and, more important, why!'

For an answer Mike Capstaff lunged clumsily.

5
Mike Capstaff's Last Trick

The man wasted no time. Seemingly he had some confidence in his ability to fight with his fists. Or maybe he had been used to thinking his weight was all-important in a rough-house. He suddenly rushed at Jack Griffin. His fists windmilled but the younger and more lithe man easily avoided the slashing blows.

Then Jack began to implement his threats. He rammed a right-hand punch into the other man's eyes and felt him stagger back. Then Jack thudded at the ugly guy's nose and saw the red blood appear.

Hurt, Capstaff went backwards, almost scattering the fire. then as he bellowed his rage, he threw himself in again. This time he was lucky. His arms wrapped around Jack Griffin in a bear-hug. This seemed to be the outlaw's idea of fighting, as if to crush his man, and not to swap punches.

Jack got out of the lousy embrace by ramming a free fist into the man's belly which slackened the bear grip a good deal. He then swiftly rammed a fist-full of knuckles into the man's mouth, saw lips split and spurt red. It was a hateful fight. But he wanted to smash this man and ultimately make him talk. He wanted to make him talk hard about Bertram Wast and the murders that had been done.

His fists once more ground into leathery flesh and Capstaff howled his rage and pain. Ezra darted out of the way, to the other side of the fire, where weird shadows flickered on the cave wall as this malevolent fight continued.

Then Jack rammed out a one-two-three-four sequence of blows that made the killer hiss and suck in breath wih pain as they landed on his face and pumped out more blood. Capstaff went back to the cave wall, spitting blood and filth and cursing this man who was besting him. Then with some speed his hand reached down and grasped a loose rock from the cave floor. As Jack moved in again, fist-fighting, the ugly man rammed the rock into Jack's face.

God, it hurt! Blood streaked hot and sweetly down Jack's face. Sure, the blow had hurt. A rock the size of a brick ramming into flesh was no joke. Jack Griffin backed as any man might.

Then, despite his tiring, night-long ride, he was swinging blows wih savage force at the outlaw's face.

Ram! 'One for Tom Mortimer, you bastard!' Jack yelled. Smash! Smash' Two blows into flesh and bone!

Capstaff was taking punishment and his belly was not used to this kind of attack although the blows had landed on his face. His guts were swirling in a mess, churning as he tried to cover his face with his leathery hands.

But the guy recovered for some seconds and swung at Jack Griffin and landed his big fists in the sheriff's face. Jack spat sweat and blood and cleared his eyes.

The fight went on in the red glare of burning brushwood. They were two men full of hate for each other, Jack Griffin feeling justification but Capstaff simply full of rage. Back and forward they fought, scattering the fire, barely able to see each other. Ezra was a grim-eyed old witness. He was surprised that Capstaff had lasted so long.

As for the sheriff, he had almost forgotten his original purpose in starting this fight. He had to remind himself that he wanted the outlaw to talk.

Capstaff tried a few dirty tricks. He kicked out but Jack knew this was coming and side-stepped, but then the outlaw tried his bear-hug trick again, almost squeezing the air out of Jack's lungs.

Jack figured to kick out as well! He rammed his boot into Capstaff's shin hard enough to break the bone. This trick hurt the man. He howled and backed, once more enabling Jack to pound in once more with some good punches to the eyes, nose and mouth. Blood masked the man's face, giving him a wild appearance in the half-light from the scattered fire. The punches were draining Capstaff's senses. He hit the cave wall again and then began to slide down like an ugly sack shaped like a man.

Mike Capstaff suddenly collapsed, huddled at the base of the cave wall, moaning like an abject imitation of a man. But Jack Griffin watched him carefully. In the past he had seen men feign defeat and then launch a surprise attack.

Blood blotched the man's evil face. This was the murderer defeated. This was a man who had asked for all he had got.

Jack Griffin was gasping for air as he rocked on his feet. Then Ezra stepped up and emptied a drinking-pan of cold water over his head! Jack's vision cleared as the water streamed down his face.

He bent forward and grabbed at Mike Capstaff again. The man was defeated but he was not unconscious. He was just a pain-filled hellion unwilling to get up. However Jack hauled him up and propped him against the cave wall. 'Talk!'

'The hell with yuh!'

'That's where you are bound, dirt!'

'Why did Wast want Tom and Sam killed?' Jack Griffin forced words out of his hurt and bleeding mouth.

'I don't know.'

The answer was rapped out viciously. Jack hit the man on his bloodied face without mercy. 'You must know, damn you!'

'I tell you I don't!' But the retort was a half-scream, proving that the outlaw had been hurt and didn't want much more.

So Jack Griffin hit him again! 'Did Wast hire you to kill them?'

'Damn yuh! Don't hit me! Sure – sure!'

'Why?'

'He said he wanted a new sheriff and deputy in the town!'

'Once again why? Give! Talk!'

'He didn't tell me everything, that hard-faced cuss. He was just the boss, with the dinero. All I got to know was that Mortimer and Brant wouldn't take orders. What sort of orders, I dunno.'

'Pretty grim ones, I guess,' snapped Jack.

'I had to get rid of Mortimer. First I picked a fight with Brant. Then I jest rode into town again. I found Tom Mortimer in the saloon. I just triggered an' got out mighty fast. There weren't many men to shake off, as I'd thought, an' I trusted Wast to discourage riders from lightin' out after me. I just headed for the hills.'

'You and the hills! You're like some rat.'

Capstaff wiped his mouth. 'The hell with you! Wast will deal with you, tin-badge.'

'I figure Wast wants the Round-O land. Now do you have any information about that? Why does the man want that ranch?'

'Don't know a blamed thing,' sneered the outlaw.

Jack stretched out a hand to Ezra. 'Give me one of my guns, pard!'

Ezra had been holding Jack's gun-belt, ready for him to strap on again now that the fight was over. Ezra handed over the gun.

Capstaff inched back. 'I've told you all I know.'

Jack held the gun-butt close to the man's face while he gripped the ruffian's shirt with his other hand. 'You are going into town with us and you're going to talk to the right people, men of some standing in the town. Make a false move and I'll gun-whip you – and then maybe shoot you.'

'I'm no good to you dead!'

'A slug in the guts hurts, hell-bent! Wal, I sure figured you knew more than you've so far told me, but never mind. You can testify that Bertram Wast ordered you to kill Tom and Sam. That makes Wast an accessory to murder. That's plenty to go along with!'

He flung the outlaw against the cave wall and then he stepped back and buckled on his gun-belt. Ezra chuckled. 'We hittin' the trail back to town. I'd like some more whiskey.'

Jack shook his head and grinned through split lips. 'Nope. We eat! Tarnation, you can't ride all night an' then all day on an empty gut! I've got some beans and I reckon this bastard has some grub cached seeing he's so fond of livin' in a cave. We set an' eat, Ezra. But first we tie this rannigan's hands behind his back.'

There was rope beside Mike Capstaff's saddle and bedroll, which he had stacked at the back of the cave.

The outlaw's hands were made secure while his eyes glittered with rage. But with a gun pointed at him, he was helpless. Then Jack and Ezra set about getting some grub inside them. Ezra went out into the dark canyon and fetched the horses along. While he was gone, Jack used some fresh water that Capstaff had stored. He used the outlaw's can to heat the water. He also used the water in another can to clean up his hands and face. These chores completed, he felt better and watched the captive struggle with the rope on his wrists.

Then Ezra returned. 'I've seen this galoot's hoss ground-hitched outside. Brought our own critturs along, too, for safety.'

'Nothing up here, pard, but an odd rattler. All right, *segundo*, sit and eat.'

Jack went through the food knowing there would be a long and tiring ride before them, with the heat of the day once they reached the flat Panhandle, and that a rumbling belly was no fun. Better one filled with beans, if nothing else!

With a prisoner on the long ride back, they'd need to be alert, and they would have to find some water in the hills for the horses and themselves before crossing the flat Panhandle territory. Finally, Jack rose and jammed Capstaff's hat on his head. 'You'll need that. Don't want you dyin' of heatstroke. We're movin' out.'

When they got into the deep-walled canyon and prepared the horses, the sky had lightened a great deal and sunrise was on the way. And, strangely, the air seemed quite cool. They knew the day would really warm up before long.

Ezra saddled the outlaw's horse. Under the muzzle of a gun, the outlaw was made to hit the saddle leather. Jack watched the man carefully in case the guy figured to spur his animal and make a break, which would be a futile play because the land was not suitable for fast riding. In any case, Capstaff knew he wouldn't get far.

But the killer outlaw sat his cayuse like a grim brooding person. His cunning brain was undoubtedly turning over the possibilities of getting out of this trap, thinking ahead to the time when maybe Wast would help him. Wast would do something to avoid his man meeting a hang-noose party.

They rode out of the twisted canyon, a party of three, each with his own thoughts. Judging by Ezra's few cackling remarks, his mind was set on drinking whiskey at an early date! Jack thought grimly of his future. With a confession from Capstaff, a written statement of his murders, he would be bound to arrest Bertram Wast if the proof was there. That would cause a stir in the town because the rancher had some influence and some pals. He even had ranch-hands who would lie on oath if paid enough. But Jack would pursue Wast hard enough. But he was up against a powerful man, a hard-case who knew friends like Judge Tarrant.

Everything led back to the insistent question. Why did Wast want men like Tom Mortimer and Sam Brant removed from this world? Why did Bertram Wast, who was wealthy enough, want Ern Spiceland's poor quality land?

There was no satisfactory answer even on the most fanciful basis. But Wast was no fool. He had strong reasons for hiring ruffians like Mike Capstaff to do his dirty work.

For some long weary hours the horses plodded on through the broken country, passing gullies and arroyos filled wih a lot of octilla, cholla and saguara cacti. This was the semi-desert country, terrain no good to the rancher, the home of jackrabbits and snakes.

Jack found water in this broken country, a basin in some rock full of discoloured liquid. The horses managed to skim some clear water from the pool but the riders still had some decent stuff to drink in their canteens. Only Ezra grumbled. 'Hell, don't it make yuh think of good American whiskey!'

'I've heard that Scotch whiskey is the best,' laughed Jack. 'But I'm no hard drinking galoot.'

They plodded on, finding a smoother trail in the foothills which made the journey a little easier for horses and men. Capstaff sagged in his saddle, hardly an elegant rider, brooding it seemed. Then they stopped when the heat of the day increased significantly and brought out the stink of saddle sweat from the animals. The men slid to the ground and stretched their legs. The wanted outlaw squatted in the scant shade of a small rock, leering contemptuously when Jack wiped sweat from his neck with his bandanna. Jack nodded curtly to Ezra and pointed into the heat-hazed distance. 'We're gettin' into the Panhàndle soon. There'll be no shade at all in that flatland, and no water.'

'Wal, we is nearer to Greenlands an' thet whiskey!'

'Don't you ever think of anything else? Right now I'd settle for some good black coffee.'

'All you'll get, Mister blasted Sheriff, is a slug in the guts!' Capstaff suddenly snarled.

Jack did not answer the surly man. But he said to Ezra: 'You'll get a reward for helping to catch a wanted baddy!'

'That's real dandy. I want a grubstake so as I can get my mule back into them hills an' look for gold.'

'Mad old bastard!' snarled Capstaff. 'There ain't no gold around here! You've got to get up among the Guadalupes to find gold in Texas!'

'Guess you're wrong,' rapped back the old-timer. 'I've seen the signs I tell yuh. I aim to stick right here and find me a bonanza in these hills. Yessir, there's a lode somewheres around these hills.'

For answer Capstaff whipped with surprising speed to his feet and rushed towards Ezra. He bundled into the old-timer and thudded a fist at the prospector's face. Ezra went down instantly.

Jack Griffin was close to the outlaw in seconds and heaved him to one side and then slammed a hard blow to the guy's jaw. The surly man staggered back, halted on the balls of his feet and teetered, glaring at the sheriff. 'I'll get you some day, you pig's dung!'

'Hit the saddle!' yelled Jack. 'I'm taking you into town and a cell!'

Later they rode over the Panhandle country. The tree-less waterless land stretched for miles, covered in tuft grass, shale and mesquite. And somewhere beyond the horizon was the start of the open range where the grass grew thick and sweet because of the winter rains. This was the location of the Bar-K ranch, where Bertram Wast held power and wanted more.

When they finally rode into town, the sight of the three riders brought folks from the stores and saloon and stopped people on the boardwalks. They all stared at the three riders, the sheriff, Capstaff and the oldish prospector.

'That's Mike Capstaff! The wanted man!' the whisper seemed to surge from one person to another. There were rough cries of approval from many male throats. A lot of folks had liked Tom Mortimer and his deputy, Sam Brant. The word had got around that Capstaff had killed them. In a land where sudden death at the end of a flaming Colt was nothing new, the thought of pure cold murder was grimly resented. Many a man might die in a fair fight but a murder had no sympathy.

Jack Griffin got his man behind the bars of a cell in the sheriff's office as quickly as possible while folks gathered and stared at the building. Then the horses were sent to the livery for a well-earned feed and rest.

Jack paced the office in a sullen thoughtful mood for a while, feeling tiredness creep over his whole body, and then there was a knock on the outer door of the building. He found Jane Spiceland waiting to greet him. Her clear eyes glanced at his taut frame, his dusty gear and the lines of fatigue among the cuts and bruises on his cheeks and jaw. 'Mister Griffin, you need attention!'

He grinned thinly. 'Just seeing you, Jane, is a tonic.'

'But those bruises!'

'Yeah – I must look a sight! But I've got good news. Come into this other room. We're too near to that filthy hombre in the cell.'

'I've heard you've brought Capstaff in. The whole town knows. My, but you need something hot to eat and drink.'

And like a woman with a man she busied herself with the stove. While Jack washed and tried to spruce himself into a presentable male close to a pretty woman, she cooked some food for him. He ran a hand over his chin and figured it was a pity he had not shaved. Still, beards and whiskers were the norm for most men in the West!

He sat down to a quickly-prepared meal, smiling at Jane, appreciating the sight of a trim waist and nicely rounded figure. She wore a check skirt and white blouse, so immaculate after the dust and sweat he had encountered during the day. She looked like an angel – and she knew how to rustle up appetising grub. He forgot his tiredness.

'You look lovely, Jane!'

'My, my! Thank you, sir!'

Ezra returned and stopped the compliments. The man had been seeing to the horses and to himself. He had bought a bottle of whiskey!

'Set, eat and put that bottle away,' said Jack sternly.

'Sure, always figured bacon and beans went well with likker!' grumbled the old-timer.

Jack had his problems to puzzle out. His next move was to confront Bertram Wast but maybe this could not be rushed because he needed to have his evidence clear and straight. He needed some sort of signed confession from Capstaff, one that could be checked and verified. Even if the hunted outlaw implicated Bertram Wast in the planning of the murders, the accusation would have to be backed with strong evidence. It might all be too much for a frontier-town sheriff! And Wast had a friend in Judge Tarrant, a man well-versed in legalities.

Maybe if Mike Capstaff stopped a red-hot slug in his gut the whole business would be solved. But who would supply the slug?

Jack and Ezra went into the office and Jane came along in spite of the fact that Jack wanted her to keep free of the whole dirty business. Breathing the same air as this wanted man was not for the girl, he thought! The killer was dirt. He didn't want Jane among dirt!

Jack began to draw up a written confession for Capstaff to sign. As the man could not write much more than his name, it wasn't much use expecting him to write it out. Evan Ezra looked on in admiration as Jack slowly scrawled the statement on thick white paper with a rough steel nib in a pen.

'Goldarn it, never thought you was a scholar, Sheriff!'

'I went to school.'

'Hell, more'n I done! Anyways, don't see what good writin' is for a galoot looking for gold in a dried-up ravine!'

Jack read the statement to the outlaw. He and Ezra sat in the cell with the man, the old-timer with a gun in his hand and grinning continuously.

'That right?' Jack demanded of the man. 'Wast paid you to kill Tom Mortimer and Sam Brant for reasons you don't know?'

'You wrote that down, huh?'

'It's here for you to sign – and much more. I've read it out to you.'

'I ain't sayin' anythin'.'

The sheriff's face set. 'You confessed to that back in the hills.'

'You can go to hell! This ain't the hills. You can't beat me up in this town. I got rights. I ain't sayin' anything an' I ain't signing your lousy bit of paper!'

And suddenly the man made a vicious lunge at the sheet of paper which Jack held but the sheriff was too fast for him. He slammed Capstaff back to the bunk on which he had sat. 'All right, bastard! You don't eat from now on. You'll sign the confession pretty damn soon.'

'I want to see Wast.'

Jack walked to the cell door with Ezra. 'If you think Wast will help you, you've got it wrong. He'll want to wash his hands of a shit like you. I might be wrong, but I think you're a liability to a man like Bertram Wast.'

'You'll swing from a cottonwood sure as you're a mangy polecat!' added Ezra in delight.

They left the cell and the cursing man sitting on the bunk. Until the man signed the confession, or made his illiterate mark on it, there wasn't much Jack could do but wait. There were pleasanter things to do, like escorting Jane back to her hotel and engaging in small talk like any man with a pretty woman!

He was not away from the sheriff's office for long. The news was around the town that the outlaw was locked up and there were maybe men in town who actually wanted to help the hellion. So he was not taking many chances. He had left Ezra in charge.

When he entered the law office again, Jack spoke to the old-timer. 'Are you too tired to do another ride for me?'

'I kin ride to hell an' back!'

Jack grinned. 'Not that far this time! I want Ern Spiceland. After all, he's my deputy and maybe he can give me some new ideas as to how to deal with this Capstaff hombre apart from starving him into submission. Get him to ride into town – fast as possible. He'll be interested to know I've got this wanted man.'

'I'm on my way!'

'You'll find a roan in the livery. Tell the jigger there I've loaned you the hoss.'

'Sure was born in the saddle,' boasted Ezra.

'Wal, git. I've got to sit here an' see no galoot gets ideas of freeing that cuss in the cell.'

The brassy afternoon sun was setting when Ezra rode out of town on Jack's roan. The old-timer rode like a proud rannigan on a horse that could eat up the miles. Ezra went down the trail in a cloud of dust, feeling young again.

Left alone the sheriff returned to the office and made sure the cell was secure. He made another attempt to get Capstaff to sign the confession statement but the hell-bent simply snarled his refusal.

'Suit yourself, you in-bitten cuss!' grunted Jack. 'But you're in a bad fix.'

Jack had callers in the next hour. Doc Turner came along and peered at the outlaw man. 'Sure reckon you'll swing. I can't prescribe medicine for what's ailing you!'

Two other citizens entered the office, vetted by Jack Griffin.

'A dirty coyote!' hissed one man. 'I seen him shoot Tom Mortimer an' you can call on me for a witness, Sheriff.'

Jack watched warily. The men stamped out, probably on their way to the Red Pine or some other saloon to enlarge upon what they had seen. The publicity might be good or bad, depending, because Wast would learn that the outlaw had been captured and that was a situation he would not like.

Jack had some peace for a few minutes and then suddenly there came a furious banging on the outside door of the building. Jack rose quickly, went to the door with a Colt in his hand. An oldish guy who was full of drink waved his hands in drunken excitement.

'There's a durned rumpus goin' on at the Packhorse! There's an ornery Mex in there shootin' up the place! The man seems a bit crazy!'

Jack did not need the drink-fuddled man to tell him something was going on down at the Packhorse Hotel. He could hear the sound of shots and the crash of breaking glass. Jack gritted his teeth and glanced back at the office, in a quandary. Dare he leave his prisoner?

He had almost decided he could not when he heard the sound of a woman screaming from that direction. The shrill sound was feminine, no doubt, and somehow he connected the scream with Jane. But the sound shrilling so piercingly in the night air could be from any woman, if there was a rumpus going on. Could be a saloon girl!

He ran out into the street, impulsively, the scream a warning to his brain. Jane was in that hotel! Maybe she was in the lounge and a crazed Mexican was triggering lead all around! But he could be wrong. Hell, he had to do something!

He went down the road at a long-legged speed and only paused when he hit the entrance to the Packhorse Hotel. And that was only to focus his eyes on the next scene.

He steadied, his Colt part of his fist almost, pointing like a menace, with his quick brain behind his trigger finger. His eyes narrowed and searching, he sighted the leering, drink-mad Mexican. The man was standing at a reception counter, swaying, incredibly drunk, a gun in each hand. He was a swarthy man, coated with range dirt. He was too fuddled with drink to use a gun with any accuracy but of course any random slugs from his flame-spitting guns could kill a person.

There was a woman in a corner of the lounge but she was not Jane Spiceland, he saw with relief. Still, the woman was scared, watching the Mex and screaming at intervals. She was maybe the wife of a visiting cattleman because her dress did not indicate saloon girl. All this in seconds came to Jack's gaze. The woman shrank to a padded seat in a corner when Jack walked forward, gun in hand.

The drunk had emptied his guns in a wild orgy, hitting no human being. The man tried to reload his twin guns but dropped shells on the linoleum-covered floor as he swayed in drink. But he got some slugs into his Colts and was therefore a menace as he stood, rocking on his feet, almost ready to fall down, attempting to sing some guttural song in Spanish.

Jack went forward, wary, not wishing to die but impelled to do something. 'Cut it out, yuh blamed fool! Drop those blasted guns! Pronto!'

For answer, the greaser whipped the weapons around and triggered wildly, bawling some stupid oaths in Spanish.

Jack momentarily wondered if he had been fed drink deliberately and put up to this display of bawling and shooting!

Jack used his gun knowing he could not take any risks with a man firing like crazy. Jack's Colt roared and spat flame. The slug whistled across the intervening space of the hotel lounge in a split second and hit the Mexican, exploding in his chest.

This had been a lightning reaction on Jack Griffin's part. No man argued wih death!

The crazy Mex went backwards under the heavy impact of the .45 bullet and crashed to the floor. The boards shook with the thud. The body twitched once, then sprawled and blood seeped quickly to the hotel floor.

The Mexican's shots had made holes in the ceiling and that was all. As the body lay on the floor and the odour of blood seemed to tinge the air, men came out of hiding, from behind chairs, the bar, tables and sofas.

Jack holstered his gun grimly. Why was death always so near to him? What kind of gruesome fate had pushed this crazy guy into his path? God, was this job really worth the candle? Maybe he should quit and buy his ranch and live peacefully.

Jack walked slowly over to the lady in the corner, who was in a faint, and at the same time Jane Spiceland came rushing out of a door and straight into his arms!

'Oh, my goodness – are you all right, Jack?'

He grinned, held her for a moment, strangely savouring the softness of her supple body. 'Yeah, I'll be all right – but maybe I need a stiff drink!'

'This is awful,' she gasped. 'This town – and you as sheriff – you're in danger!'

'Nothing I can't handle, with luck and God's help, Jane.'

'That *awful man*!'

He lost his grin. 'I reckon he was put up to it! Seems kinda strange. And I know I've left Mike Capstaff in that durned cell unguarded! Hell!'

He stiffened for a second with the urgent thought. The girl wondered for a moment about what was in the mind of this tall lean range-man with the wary eyes which could, nevertheless, crinkle into a ready smile, something she loved to see!

Then without a word Jack turned and moved with long strides to the outside door of the hotel. He thrust on and on, went with urgency to the road, something nagging in his brain. He saw only Capstaff, the wanted man, his captive who deserved justice and punishment.

He reached the office door and went in with angry strides, angry at his own stupidity. Sure as hell the Mex had been a setup job. It seemed too damned coincidental.

He never finished his furious thoughts. He opened

the cell door where Mike Capstaff lay on his bunk. Jack's gun was again in his hand for he had seen variations of this trick before. But this was no trick. Capstaff was not lying doggo, ready to leap up when the cell door opened.

The outlaw would never try another trick! Never! A man needed guts to try tricks.

Someone had entered the unlocked sheriff's office while the row at the Packhorse was in progress and shot Capstaff clean through the head. A gun had been poked through the locked cell door and a couple of shots had done the deadly work.

The man's head was a mess of red blood where a gory hole had been made. The killer had been able to draw a bead on the man as he lay on his bunk and the sheriff had been tricked into investigating a rumpus.

As Jack Griffin stared, he knew full well the identity of the man who had bested him. Bertram Wast had scored!

With the confession unsigned, it would be difficult to pin anything on the rancher. Wast had stopped any possibility of Mike Capstaff implicating him in the murder of Tom Mortimer and Sam Brant.

To hell and damn with Bertram Wast! How could he defeat this wealthy, unscrupulous man?

6
Ezra Rides Alone

There was no need to worry about the prisoner now! Dead badmen were no problem. With this thought, Jack went over to his desk and folded the unsigned confession and put it away. Then, with things on his mind, he went out into the street and headed for the Packhorse Hotel although he was damned bone tired.

The manager had already summoned Doc Turner to deal with the dead Mexican. A man was busy sweeping up broken glass. Jack drew the manager to one side. 'Got any ideas as to how and why this dead hombre started all this?'

The manager shook his head. 'As a rule we don't allow Mexicans in this place. He just appeared, full of drink. Gawd, this town is getting worse!'

Jack went up to Doc Turner. 'I'm sure raisin' business for you an' the undertaker. There's another corpse back in the cell.'

'You don't mean –'

'Sure do. That rumpus with the Mexican was set up just to get me out of the way. Capstaff was paid to kill Tom Mortimer and the deputy and the man who paid Capstaff for his ungodly work also killed him.'

'You've got your work cut out, Sheriff. For me, I'm

an old galoot and getting mighty tired of dead men.'

'Wal, just for the records which you an' the undertaker are supposed to keep about the characters bent for Boothill, I had to shoot a rogue out by the buttes the other day,' drawled Jack. 'I buried him there – galoot by the name of Red Holbin. He was in Wast's pay and layin' for me.'

'Red Holbin, huh?' barked the Doc. 'Another villain, I guess. Well, you can get on with killing them all for me! Wast, huh? Never did like that gent! Too much ego.'

'Huh? What's that?'

Doc Turner smiled. 'Too damned greedy and self-important, Sheriff.'

Tired and wishing he could get his head down, Jack Griffin nevertheless pushed himself on and on. He went to a saloon in the hope of finding information about the Mexican. Maybe there was a man who had known the galoot personally. Maybe there was a lead to be had here.

In the second saloon he found the bartender who had served the dead man. 'Yeah, I remember him. I knew him, too. Usually he never had much dinero an' this was the only saloon in town where they would serve him. Must ha' got some dollars from somewhere. He paid for a lot of cheap whiskey an' slung it down his throat.'

'Did you see any other rannigan with him – a white man?'

'Nope. He was drinking solitary.'

So there was no proof that Wast had been near the man! Well, the idea had been worth pursuing. Jack went out into the evening air again and realised he'd been on his feet too long and was tired. A man was busy lighting kerosene lanterns in the main drag.

As Jack reached his office, he saw Doc Turner with two men who were carrying a bag with a body in it.

'Reckon you don't want him around as an ornament,' drawled the Doc. 'So these guys are taking the cadaver to Boothill right now. You want to witness a burial party?'

'Not durned likely. I'm really played out, Doc.'

With Doc Turner's cackling laugh in his ears, Jack went into his quarters to rest. Real fatigue was setting in, although if any emergency arose he could drive his frame on for a long time. It had been this way in his bounty-hunting days. But he felt he was entitled to rest as some sort of insurance for the future.

But Ezra was late. Jack glanced at the big clock on the wall. What was keeping the old-timer?

As if in answer to his thoughts he heard the sound of boots on the boardwalk outside his window. He heard Ezra Hide's high-pitched voice as he argued with someone. Then Ezra and Ern Spiceland walked into the room. The oldster pointed dramatically at Jack who was lying on his bunk.

'Can yuh beat that! Takin' it easy while I ride the skin offen my rear end! How about that, Mister Ern?'

Jack rolled upright. 'Set down and get that bottle out!'

The oldish prospector lowered himself to a chair as if his joints would hardly bend. His beady eyes flicked in the direction of the cells. 'Where is he?'

Jack glanced at him grimly. 'Capstaff's dead.'

'You kilt him dead! Heh! Heh!'

'I did not. A certain hombre walked in here and shot the jigger all to hell! I reckon they've just finished burying him out on Boothill.'

And Jack Griffin told Ern and Ezra all about the rumpus at the Packhorse Hotel. 'I wanted you to work on that outlaw, Ern. You might have got him to sign that confession – but he's dead now so that is that, except to discover who actually shot him. It was murder, outlaw or not.'

'I sure hope Jane was safe at the Packhorse.'

'She's fine and prettier than ever.'

Ern grinned at the remark. 'Wal, sure seems I've had my ride for nothin'. Guess I'll have to stay in town overnight. As your deputy, what about lettin' me have some floor space in this calaboose? I got a bedroll on my horse.'

'Sure. Unless you want to sample the comforts of the Packhorse.'

'Listen, Jack, I can't afford such luxuries. I got a mortgage on my spread an' those longhorns are plenty lean.'

Old Ezra began to cackle suddenly. He lifted his bottle and gulped at the raw liquid. Then he patted the bottle affectionately and made his remark. 'He ain't got the grass.'

'What's that supposed to mean?' Jack grinned at the prospector.

'Not much grass up at that ranch – that's all.'

'You don't have to tell me that,' said Ern Spiceland.

'Is there some significance behind that cryptic remark, Ezra?' Jack stared at the man.

'Ain't no grass! Might be somethin' else – but it ain't grass.'

Jack smiled and shook his head dubiously at the old man. 'That booze is too strong for your weak old brain, Ezra!'

'I seen the signs!' cackled Ezra and he shook his head as if his inward thoughts amused him. Finally his eyes closed and he fell asleep in the chair. 'Loco,' muttered Jack.

'Yeah. Listen, I think I'll run over an' talk with sister Jane for a while.'

'I've got to hit the hay.'

'Sure. Mighty fine gal is my sister Jane.'

'Yup. Mighty pretty.'

'Got brains and book learnin'.'

'You're right, Ern.' Jack laughed. 'You figure I got a chance?'

'Maybe you have. Yeah, mebbeso.'

'I might have a better chance with Jane if I hung up my guns an' bought that spread.'

Ern Spiceland went out of the building with a slight smile on his lips. Jack locked the door and partly undressed, got into the bunk in his quarters and promptly fell into a deep sleep, something that had been clawing into his brain for some time.

Ezra sprawled on his wood chair, the bottle of rot-gut on a table before him. In the town there was roaring activity in the saloons with honky-tonk pianos hammering away. An hour later Jack had to get up again as Ern thumped on the outer door. Then there was silence as tired men slept soundly – with guns not far away!

From force of habit the men wakened with the dawn and the sound of wheels and horses in the street. Silently they sluiced with cold water and then made breakfast, bacon, beans and flapjacks.

'Jane is goin' out to the ranch with me this morning,' said Ern. 'You care to ride out, Jack? Unless you got pressing business in town.'

'No dead men today, I hope!' The sudden idea of riding along with Jane was appealing. Somehow her presence seemed mighty important, like knowing she was there to look at and talk to.

'I reckon I'll go along with you, Mister Spiceland,'

Ezra suddenly said eagerly. 'Kinda like the looks of your land, sir!'

'Hell, you do! Then you're the only feller around here that does. Exceptin' Bertram Wast maybe.'

'Heh! Heh!' Ezra started to cackle mysteriously.

They rode out of town slowly that morning, Jack on his roan and Ezra on a horse fresh from the livery at the rear of the sheriff's office. Ern had his own mount. Jane was riding a proud pinto.

Jack found he was able to ride alongside Jane most of the way, she looking charmingly lovely on the horse. She wore blue jeans tucked into riding boots and a buckskin jacket over her red shirt. With a wide-brimmed hat over her corn-coloured hair, she was a dazzling picture for any red-blooded male. Most women in Greenlands or on the surrounding ranches rode mounts side-saddle or travelled by buckboard. Jane seemed marvellous modern!

Jack was so pleased at being so close to the girl he began to wish he could touch her, hold her, a mad thought seeing she kept herself at a distance so far.

He realised he had no real need to ride out to the Round-O ranch. He just wanted to be close to Jane!

'Maybe I'll get myself that Box-T spread, Jane,' he suddenly remarked. 'It ain't right that a man should go around with a gun against other men all his years.'

'You want to settle out here?'

He looked directly into her clear blue eyes. 'Sure. Seems to me a man should get himself some roots, and this is cattle land. And, Jane, when I get that ranch –' He paused.

She looked away, at her horse's bobbing head, and then she turned to him as if unafraid to show the soft lights in her eyes.

'When I get that ranch and a house with it, I'd sure

be pleased if you'd come over and tell me how you like it. Because that's mighty important.'

'Is it, Jack?'

'Yep. Because I reckon to build that house the way you'd like it.'

Suddenly he felt the ride out had not been wasted time!

The sun climbed steadily and heated the dusty trail, a well-used track across the undulating land where cattle herded in the distance. Then they brisked the animals to a canter and crossed valleys and flat-lands quickly in an attempt to cut down on time in the saddle.

When they rode into the ranch-yard, Bandy Manners and Fred Spiceland came to meet them, ceasing work on the chores they had in hand. The four riders climbed down. Ezra led the animals to the feed corral.

'You know something,' bawled Bandy. 'I seen Bar-K riders up in the hills this morning.'

'Were they on our range?' asked Ern curiously.

'Yep. They didn't see me. Wast was with them an' that ramrod, Otto Tribe. There was two other range hands, no-accounts, I guess.'

'What were they up to?' Jack felt suddenly suspicious.

'I figger they was looking for them long-horns.'

And Bandy started to laugh uproariously. He was wearing sheepskin chaps and he slapped them with a horny hand. 'Them jiggers won't find them beeves. I got them hidden in a queer kinda canyon. Take more than a mornin' of ridin' around to locate those critturs.'

Ezra Hide heard Bandy's last remark. 'Maybe they weren't looking fer cows! Maybe they got somethin' else in mind.'

Bandy Manners had met Ezra last night and was

now fully acquainted with the eccentric old-timer. As a matter of fact, the two men were similar types, except that Bandy had spent his years herding cattle and Ezra had drifted to searching for gold.

'What in tarnation would those galoots be lookin' for?' demanded Bandy. 'Only cows an' brush up there.'

'Mebbeso. Sure thing, you maybe right,' Ezra hastily replied.

'Crazy as a coot,' muttered Bandy. 'Sure is one thing about steers. They don't send a man crazy. Plenty o' sense in cows. Kin eat 'em, too!'

Jane had entered the ranch-house, and watching her go Jack Griffin was about to follow with the idea of talking about the desirability of a good ranch-house, when he felt Ezra tug at his sleeve.

'I been thinking. You've treated me right fine an' I'm an old man. I figure you ought to along with me – maybe into them hills.'

'Why, old-timer?'

'Kin you tell me if'n that broken country lies in the Round-O title?'

'Sure it does but I don't rightly know the exact borders. Reckon Ern could tell you. What's on your mind?'

'Aw, just things – signs in that broken terrain. Let's go see Ern – iffen you won't ride out with me.'

Ern Spiceland was inspecting some new carpenter work around by the side of the ranch-house, where the timber had been burnt, when Ezra and Jack strolled up.

'This oldster wants to know about your borders in the broken country,' Jack grinned.

Ern turned. 'Since you ask, old-timer, I'll tell you. I got title to the land that extends ten miles or more into that cussed country an' I wish there was as much grass out there as there is in the Bar-K range. No real grass. Just canyons, buttes and brush. Can't help figuring that the brush will spread someday right down to this good range and then it will be goodbye to ranching. Can't feed cattle on cholla cactus and catsclaw.'

'How come you got all that land?'

'Hell, it was in with the title. Had to take the lot or leave it. Guess it must ha' been passelled up that way when the Injuns sold it to the Administration. Anyway, if you really want to know everything, I've got my title deed with a copy lodged in the County Courthouse at Abilene. An' there's stakes out there in the broken country marking my borders. I put them stakes here myself.'

'You sure told me everythin',' muttered Ezra.

He walked away and hitched one leg on the rail of a fence and stared at the blurred hills in the distance.

Jack grinned at Ern Spiceland. 'Funny old cuss but I like him.'

'Sure. He can stick around here if he likes. Certainly taking more than a passin' interest in my land, though.'

After some half-hour of staring at the horizon, Ezra suddenly decided he would go riding alone. He went for his horse. The animal was already saddled and there was a rifle stuck in the saddle holster. With a wave of his hand and not a word of explanation, he was off.

Jack Griffin knew he was heading for the wild broken country but as to why he hadn't a clue.

But as Jack watched the old-timer gallop off, he had an odd inward kind of hunch. Too late, he realised he had not fully questioned Ezra about his reasons for wanting to ride out to the buttes and rocky lands on the outskirts of Ern's borders. What was really behind the old-timer's many questions about the ranch's borders?

And then the inward hunch became a hard, startling question in his mind, his brain sifting the many crazy ideas. But this kind of thinking about the broken country and Ezra's curiosity was preposterous. Ezra was touched by the sun, too many hard days in the saddle and loneliness. It was silly to take any account of the man's cracked ideas. Surely Ezra was like all old prospectors, a bit loco!

And yet, as Jack stared at the tiny dot which was Ezra on the horizon, he felt he ought to go after the strange old guy, ask more questions and get to understand what was on his mind. After all, Ezra had originally asked him to ride out.

Jack Griffin told Ern Spiceland. 'I'm a-goin' after that ornery old galoot. Don't rightly know why. Tell Jane. I'll be back.'

Jack got his dependable roan from the corral, talked to the crittur and breathed sounds into its nostrils and the animal edged close to him. He had some affinity with the horse, he felt.

As he rode out, he noticed the poor quality of the grass and, in places, the downright lack of it. There were many patches of shale and Ern Spiceland was right, the brush was growing into the land. Even cholla cactus was springing up. Cactus was bad. Too much and it would cover a lot of land in a few years. Every season, the cactus spread spores over a wide area.

But soon his thoughts turned to Ezra again. He had lost sight of the man, probably around the first of the buttes. But Jack had a pretty good idea of the general direction Ezra had taken. He rowelled the roan into a brisk canter, conscious of the sun-heat on his back.

He rode fast over the ground, avoiding small rocks, clumps of cholla and ridges of outcrop rock. This land wasn't the lush Panhandle country where cattle could find feed without moving far.

He rounded the first butte, rock rising like a big finger. He could not see any sign of Ezra. He would have to sight him soon if he wanted to talk to him now and not return to Ern's ranch after a useless ride. He slowed in an attempt to read track. He located a fresh horse hoof-print in the sand of a small depression and knew his had been made by Ezra's mount. How far ahead was the old fool! Or was he a fool? Jack pondered and then he was suddenly alert as a shot rang out.

Jack Griffin was taut in the saddle, staring all round him, his boots pressing hard against the stirrups. Even as he tensed for further sounds, there was a real rataplan of shots from just ahead. He judged it was mostly rifle fire. He rowelled his horse in the next swift second and the strong brute sprang into full gallop along the canyon.

Jack did not hear another shot. Had someone triggered more shots, he would have heard them above the drum of the roan's hoofs.

He urged the cayuse up a shale slope, breasted the ridge and sent the horse pell-mell down the other side, slithering, with hoofs digging into the loose material and the animal wide-eyed. The incline levelled out into a valley of grass, cholla and shale. There was a patch of sand at the distant end, with a horse running in uncertain circles, obviously suddenly scared.

A dark blotch sprawled on the yellow sand, motionless, a shape with arms and legs, a man.

Of course, the sprawled figure was old Ezra and the horse was the one from the ranch. Jack sent his roan up the valley in a flurry of pounding hoofs and when he got close to the body he flung himself off his mount before the animal slithered to a halt. He felt sure the attackers were not around and so he flung caution to one side and leaned over the body of the old-timer.

Sharp breath hissed in Jack's mouth when he saw the spread of red blood on the oldster's shirt. Taut lines dragged into his face when the thought of death hit his mind. Was Ezra alive?

The bullet hole was dead centre for the heart and Ezra was not breathing. Still, Jack had hope. He tore the blood-stained shirt to one side and felt for some life in Ezra's heart. But there was none, only the oozing blood and the odour of death. No one could live with a bullet hole so close to the heart. He tried another test and suddenly sat back and cradled the old guy in his arms.

Jesus hell! Death again! Was here no end to it! And then he realised how much he had got to like the old prospector and tears came to his eyes as he cursed the villains who had done this.

He stared ahead at the valley which was now a death scene for the whole awful play. He cursed the unknown men who had killed Ezra and, jumping to his feet, his hand fell to his gun butt and he crouched in the gun-fighter's stance while he glared around. But it was an empty scene, the semi-arid land wih a dead body and himself full of ugly thoughts concerning the unknown bushwhackers.

Ezra had rode into a trap, maybe an accidental one but a trap nevertheless. And right now there was no sign of men in these hills and valleys, only the endless silence which was the eternal feature. The swines who had killed Ezra were a long way off. He could not hear or see them. He dropped to the ground and placed an ear close to mother earth. There was not even a vibration of a horse's hoof. The old Indian trick of listening to the earth did not provide a clue.

Jack stood over the body, protectively, brooding. Who had killed Ezra and why? He could make a good guess as to the identity of the attackers when he recalled Bandy's remarks about seeing Bertram Wast and his hands in the hills that morning. Had Ezra fallen foul of Wast and Otto Tribe? Had they shot him?

If that was true, the next question was why had the old-timer been killed?

True, Ezra had helped Jack to capture Mike Capstaff. Maybe this was simply Wast's answer, a killer swine getting revenge.

But Jack Griffin felt dissatisfied with this explanation. Some hunch, nagging in his mind, told him that Wast would not identify himself as a murderer before his men no matter how much he trusted them. There was something else.

Jack lifted Ezra's body with the intention of placing it on the horse's back. He'd go back to town with the body. No hole in the ground for the old-timer! But in a way maybe Ezra would like to be left in the hills!

Then he noticed the way the old fellow's hand was grasped around a large chunk of rock, a bit the size of a man's fist. Curiously he placed the body down again and gently removed the rock from the clenched fist. Staring at the jagged chunk of rock, it was some seconds before the importance of the find really penetrated his mind. He examined the curious rock and then, in a flash, it was all astoundingly clear.

He knew enough about gold-bearing quartz to see that this piece was so filled with wire and flake gold that slivers of pure yellow metal could, without too much difficulty, be prised out of the stone with a knife! Gold! In these rocky hills! The rare Texas gold that many men said did not exist! So Ezra had been right!

This, then, was Bertram Wast's aim and the pivot of all his nefarious plans?

This was why he wanted Ern's ranch right up to the arid borders! This was the reason why the man had planned murder. A greedy man, he had wanted more and more.

7
Gold Canyon

It was all so clear now. Wast wanted to chase Ern Spiceland off his land so that he could step in and buy it without raising suspicion. So Wast had settled to worrying Ern in the hope that he would give up trying to raise herd on the poor grazing land. Wast had sent his men to fire the ranch-house. Wast had tried to engineer an accusation of rustling againt Ern. Any of these measures, had they succeeded, might have sickened Ern into selling and getting out.

Once Wast had the title to the land, he could file claim to all the gold-mining rights. In view of the richness of gold in the piece of quartz Ezra had clutched, it seemed that the land of the Round-O ranch was the location of the lode. This valueless territory – from the point of view of cattle-raising – was therefore potentially rich. No one suspected that there was gold in the broken country so near to the edge of the Panhandle. The very idea was laughed at. Texas was a cattle country, except for the uncharted and dreaded Guadalupes far to the west.

Jack Griffin sat still over the body of his old partner and brooded bitterly on the irony of Ezra dying with the coveted gold in his grasp. All his life the oldster had sought gold. Probably this had been a craze with him. He had been right about the signs of gold which his experienced eyes had detected in this broken country so close to the territory of Greenlands.

Why had Wast killed the old-timer?

There could be no other reason than that the lode was somewhere nearby and that Wast had seen Ezra acting suspiciously. Ezra must have been fairly sure of the location of the mother lode because he had ridden his horse straight out from the Round-O to this rocky valley. He had asked Jack to ride with him, something Jack had turned down. It seemed the old man had wanted Jack to examine the land, to check on his ideas and his finds. Apparently Ezra had been through this rocky terrain last night when he went out to seek Ern Spiceland. Maybe that was why Ezra had been late in returning.

Jack sighed grimly, knowing a lot of these ideas were necessarily conjecture but some things stood out. Ezra was dead and beyond aid. There was gold up here in this rocky, broken country and on Ern's title.

Probably Ern's title deed gave him mineral rights to the land in his borders, although Ern had probably never thought about that when signing the deed. Few men considered finding gold in this territory. It was just broken land on the edge of cattle country.

Jack rose swiftly. He had to get the dead man back to the ranch and a decent burial and he had to talk to Ern Spiceland about many things.

He carefully pocketed the quartz and then placed Ezra's body across the roan. Jack got to saddle leather and rode forward, stopping to pick up the reins of Ezra's horse. Then they cantered slowly out of the valley, heading to the Round-O location.

After a slow ride, he came within sight of the ranch buildings, squatting flat on the edge of the Panhandle country without so much as a cottonwood for shade. When the winds came, as they did every year, Ern would have to stake his ranch-house to the earth with ropes.

Jack reached the ranch and Bandy Manners and Ern came riding out furiously. They had seen the riderless horse. Jack explained it all simply. 'Wast! He or his hands shot Ezra. I found him in a rocky valley. He had exchanged shots with some rannigans afore a bullet got him. Got somethin' else mighty important to tell you, Ern, but maybe it will keep until after we bury Ezra.'

They were in the ranch-yard when Fred and Jane hurried to meet them and the girl was suddenly pale and shocked when she realised what had happened. Little muscles twitched in Fred's jaw. 'Murder! Just damned murder! Why?'

Jack held back on explanations. There was a simple, stern, yet necessary job to be done in the shape of a decent burial, right here on the open range, the way the oldster would have wished it. Jack recited a few words of service over the grave they dug. Out in the western borders a man could be buried anywhere and not always in the town Boothill.

'You've asked a few questions,' muttered Jack Griffin to the others. 'If you come into the ranch-house I'll tell you somethin' mighty important and show you why a villain name of Bertram Wast wants this land.'

Rather mystified, they walked into the living-room of the house and sat down. 'I reckon you are all interested in Ern's success with the Round-O. Bandy, you are Ern's man and you're with him. Fred and Jane – you are his brother and sister, so here goes.'

'Sounds like a council meeting,' joked Ern.

Jack grinned back. He brought out the piece of quartz rock and laid it on the table, smiling at their expressions. Ern was the first to reach out and examine the rock closely. His bright eyes flickered. 'Where did you get this, Jack?'

'I found it in Ezra's clenched fist when I found his body.'

'It's gold-bearing quartz!'

'Yeah, I reckon.'

'Out here in this territory?' Ern tried to pick out a sliver of the pure yellow metal with his thumb-nail. The flake of gold curled out and Ern Spiceland put it on the palm of his hand. 'It ain't fool's gold, huh?'

'I've seen fool's gold – a useless quartz – but this ain't that stuff, Ern. I been around with miners an' I know pure gold when I see it, although in a quartz rock, not nugget form.'

'You don't mean to tell me that oldster found gold around here?'

'Seems like that.'

'I figured he was kinda loco about the subject.'

'He wasn't so crazy. You know what this means, Ern? Ezra was killed in a rocky valley on your Round-O land. He was shot by Wast or his rannigans, sure as thunder. And he was killed because Wast knows about this gold-bearing quartz around that valley. That's the simple reason why Wast wants you off your land an' all his filthy attempts to scare you, fire you and kill people are centred around that fact. You've got the title deed to a bonanza, Ern.'

There was a hushed silence and they all stared again at the chunk of rock. Except for the streaks of yellow, it might ordinarily have attracted little attention.

'I'm no expert,' said Fred Spiceland, 'but if you believe this is gold – and a pointer to more – it explains all Bertram Wast's damnable actions. I'll have a look at your deed, Ern. Guess I'm the only lawyer around here.'

Ern went to a closet and brought out a metal strong-box. He soon brought out the parchment deed with the copper-plate quill writing. Fred read through the deed with the care of one studying law. After a few minutes he said slowly: 'You've got clear title to all minerals inside your land borders. Ordinarily, in this territory that would mean just a lot of rock and shale. Wast must have guessed this clause was in your title.'

'Unless he has seen the copy deed in Abilene,' put in Jane quickly. 'Then it wouldn't be merely a guess. Wast is influential. Look at the way he is so friendly with Judge Tarrant.'

'Could be somethin' like that,' said Fred slowly. 'Mind you, we've got to find the exact location of that gold in the valley.'

'I know where I found old Ezra,' said Jack. 'And he had that rock in his hand. Maybe that's the spot – the location.'

'We'll prospect up there.' Ern seemed to make a decision. 'We'll set up a camp but do it in secret. Gold always spells trouble. Wast won't beat me. Not if I can help it – and we'll find that gold-bearing location for old Ezra's sake.'

'Wal, we've got it pin-pointed.' Jack Griffin summed it all up. 'The next move is up to you, Ern. It's your land.' And Jack handed Ern the lump of quartz.

'Why don't we get goin' right now?' Ern Spiceland wanted to know. 'We've got some daylight left and we can make camp.' He frowned at Jane. 'I'm not so sure about you, sister, dear! Guess you'd better stay here with Fred.'

'Guess again. I'm going with you. I want to see this gold, too. And I can cook in a camp for you men.'

'All right,' growled Ern. 'But maybe Bandy an' me only will stay any length o' time in them hills and that valley in particular. Wast and his gunnies might get to snoopin' around. You might have to go back to that hotel, Jane. Can't stay out there, huh? Maybe Jack will escort you back to town?'

And Ern Spiceland threw a smiling glance at the girl. Then they moved out into the ranch-yard and for some time they were busy loading two packhorses. They loaded stakes, timber, wire and nails on to one horse. The other carried enough canvas to rig a tent or two and a box containing sticks of dynamite.

'Never know what we might want out there in the arid valley,' muttered Ern.

They set off later, a substantial party of riders, and only when they were moving out did Ern realise he was leaving the ranch-house and buildings unattended. He cursed. But it seemed he had to take some risks.

The ride to the rocky valley, past the small canyons, was not a fast journey for the loaded packhorses merely trudged along as if reluctant to make the trip at all. Some hours passed and the trek seemed laborious in the silent arid land, but presently Jack led the way over the shale hill and down into the long rocky valley where he had found the dead old prospector. The memory of this made his lips tighten. And then they found the spot where Ezra had fallen. Jack pointed without words and the others stared at the spot.

Jack began to scan the tracks around while the others sat their horses as he studied the sign. He was looking for tracks of Ezra's last footsteps. He moved far away from the middle of the valley and soon found tracks of a horse with a man's footprints alongside. The solitary tracks were significant in this rocky semi-enclosed valley, where a blue sky made a canopy and humans seemed to be the only living things.

The tracks soon brought him right up against a rocky pileup which might have been the remnants of a distant age. But Jack found enough evidence of Ezra's last trail. The old-timer had ridden his horse parallel with a rocky wall, leaving some hoof-prints in a patch of sand. Then he had moved out to the middle of the rock-girt valley. Jack wondered why. Was it because Ezra had found the quartz?

The others were some three hundred yards away, in the middle of the valley, some of the rocks brilliantly white in the direct sun. Jack waved them over. Jack stood looking down at a deep fissure that ran for some length down the floor of the valley. He thought the place was volcanic in origin, untouched by man or new movement of nature for centuries. Like all men who had pioneered the western trails, Jack knew something about gold and the tales he had heard. Some gold was found in pure nuggets, from river beds, and in other places gold had been discovered in rock, like the chunk that Ezra had found. Jack was not the old gold-hound of Ezra's ilk but he had a smattering of gold lore.

The others rode quickly over the valley and halted close to Jack Griffin. 'I'm goin' down this fissure. Ezra was around this spot, according to the tracks he made. They seem to halt here. Anyway, it's worth a looksee. Just hang around friends.'

Jack Griffin climbed down the jagged crack in the

earth, the depth of the fissure being about fifteen feet. As he slowly went down, grasping at hand-holds, he examined the nature of the rock around him. So far it was just red sandstone. There was no sign of quartz; nothing like that kind of rock. This could not be the place from where Ezra had obtained his specimen.

He climbed slowly back to the surface again and shook his head to Fred, Jane and Bandy and even as he did this negative thing he heard a shout from Ern Spiceland. 'Jack! Git yourself over here!'

Ern had lowered himself into another crevice. Jack took fast strides over to the place and stared down at Ern, deep in the jagged, rocky cleft. Then, in minutes, he joined the other on the bed of the natural cleft in the earth. Looking around the rough slot, it seemed to be mainly sand and pebbles with jagged rock forming the sides. And then he noticed the dull streaks of gold in the rocky quartz. Wind and rain over the centuries had scoured the rock to reveal the dull gleam of the yellow metal. And that was not all. The pebbles were more than rock. They were dull, rounded nuggets of pure gold, washed by rain of the bygone ages!

Ern had picked up some of the pebbles. He whipped out a knife from his belt and scraped furiously at one. 'This is gold! The bed of this fissure is thick with 'em!'

'Poor old Ezra was right!' Jack paused for some moments. 'Gold in Texas! Who would ha' believed it!'

'There's a fortune in this gash!' exclaimed Ern Spiceland. 'And on my land – my title!'

'You'll be a rich man,' said Jack slowly. 'Ezra must ha' found his lump of quartz in this cleft an' I reckon Wast or his galoots must ha' seen him gettin' out of this hole in the ground. But they couldn't have looked around. Maybe they just chased the oldster and then cut him down with a slug, damn them! They didn't figure Ezra held a secret in his hand or they'd be all over this place by now.'

Ern straightened his shoulders. 'Let's take this situation easy, Jack. This gold can wait until we set up a camp.'

Jack nodded. 'Hell, it's been here for centuries! Yeah, we can't rush at everything – although there is enough gold lyin' around in these pebbles to make a man rich. And the moment we put up a tent Wast or one of his hired hands will discover us.'

Ern held two nuggets of the dull yellow metal. 'Don't look like gold, huh? But polish or scrape it and you'll know what it is. Men will kill for a find like this! You know something? We've got to get Jane away from here.'

Jack Griffin had to agree because suddenly the discovery of the gold bonanza meant trouble with ruffians who dealt in murder just for the sake of Wast's cash handouts. What would happen if the news of gold reached these gun-happy bastards? There would be death, that was for sure!

The two men climbed out of the deep gash, easily because of the many natural foot-holds and hand-holds. The others were waiting for them at the top of the geological fault. Fred grasped Jack's shoulder. 'What's all the shouting and excitement about?'

Jack and Ern showed the other three their finds, the roundish dull nuggets which were unbelievably pure gold and the lumps of quartz full of the streaks of the precious metal. 'The bonanza is there! This is what old Ezra found, I reckon.'

Jane stared at the examples. 'Is it really gold? I'm sure I don't know.'

'The nuggets are pure gold,' said Jack. 'Centuries ago water must have washed through here and the nuggets are the result but the dull yellow streaks in the quartz are like that because the rock is so hard. That gold has to be mined and crushed and the gold extracted but the nuggets are different. Here's a real test.'

He showed them a trick he had learned years ago when he had been with some miners. He took one of the nuggets and placed it on a flat stone nearby and then he rummaged for a hammer in one of their packs. He began to hammer the nugget and it was surprising how quickly the round nugget became flattened. He beat it out until it was no thicker than a Mexican dollar.

'If it's malleable, it's gold,' he said with conviction. 'Fool's gold won't beat out. Too brittle! This is real gold!'

The whole party broke into a babble of excited conversation, making Jack Griffin smile thinly. He had seen the effect of gold on ordinary people years ago and in some instances the result was terrifying. But he felt sure Ern and Jane, Fred and Bandy would eventually take it in their stride. Then he heard something in the distance that made him yell out. 'Get those pack-horses into cover!'

'What's wrong?' This from Fred, still examining the beaten-out nugget.

'Get behind some rock! There's riders way down this valley!'

They wheeled as Jack shouted and they stared for brief seconds at the shape of horsemen riding steadily up the rock-littered valley. Then Ern and Bandy whipped around for their horses and grabbed rifles from the saddle-holsters. At the same time the whole party pulled the animals into a natural stall in the valley wall. This job took some confused minutes and the other riders came menacingly closer.

But the horses went into a small, rugged, high-walled enclosure in the valley wall and the foot of this place was littered with boulders large and small which might afford cover to men if some hard-cases started shooting. Within some fast minutes the thoughts of all in Jack's party were switched from the fascinating lure of gold to the danger of the approaching riders.

Even at a distance they could distinguish the big, black-suited figure of Bertram Wast. He sat astride a big all-black horse, like a natural enemy, a man of menace. Beside him was Otto Tribe and behind that guy were two other men, hired hands with guns, no doubt.

'Gold and death!' thought Jack Griffin. 'Sure is a true saying!'

When the horses were in the little rocky enclosure and Jane was sent to keep them from being spooked, Ern, Bandy, Fred and Jack dropped behind the bigger boulders, rifles and Colts at the ready. Fred Spiceland gulped at a situation that was not usual for him. He realised that the law of the gun was as powerful as the law of the pen. Maybe more so!

The approaching riders suddenly wheeled their mounts almost on to haunches and then went off at a tangent across the valley floor.

'Seen us!' shouted Jack Griffin. 'I figured they weren't taking much notice when they first came up! I don't think Wast expected to see us here.'

Wast led his men to a spot across the valley, finding

cover just like Jack Griffin and his party. Even so Jack could see the movement of dark-coloured men in dirty range gear and their animals across the distance of the valley. He figured they were still in range of a well-sighted rifle, but the same thing could be applied to Wast and his tough riders.

There was a sudden silence in the valley for some long moments. Men watched each other over the distance.

'I wonder what that greedy shit figures on doing?' Jack yelled to Ern, who was sprawled behind a boulder hardly five feet away.

'Guess he'd like to kill us all. That sidewinder must ha' guessed we've found the bonanza. Somehow he knew there was gold up here.'

'But not the exact location,' supplied Jack. 'He didn't know the bonanza was right here.'

'He'd ha' been picking up the gold by now iffen he'd known that!'

'Sure thing.'

Wast's voice from the other side of the valley alerted them. 'Griffin, why don't you come out and take your rightful place on the side of law and order?'

Jack Griffin yelled back. 'What the hell d'you mean, Wast?'

'You're siding with rustlers, man! My hands have found Bar-X cattle on the Round-O range.'

'You ride like blazes out here loaded with guns to tell us that?'

'I ask you to do your job as sheriff. You should arrest Spiceland and that man of his.'

'Strays, huh?'

'Nope. These critturs were re-branded, worked over brands as we say. I haven't sold any cattle to Spiceland. They're rustled stock. Now do your job,

Sheriff. Arrest those two men, Spiceland and his side-kick.'

Bandy Manners gave a muffled curse. 'He found them beeves! If I could git a bead on him he wouldn't call me a rustler!'

Jack Griffin laughed outright. 'Cut out the bluff, Wast! I know why you're out here in this broken country and it ain't on account of cattle. You want to kill Ern Spiceland an' then make a bid to claim his title deeds to this range.'

'You're talking pure crap!' Wast's voice yelled back.

'Yeah? I'm not arrestin' anyone on account of worked-over cows, and you flaming-well know it! If you want to know, I'm looking for a murderer.'

'Anyone we know?' came a guffawing voice, one of Wast's hired hands.

'Yeah – you, Wast! You or your men killed one Ezra Hide. You'll swing like a chunk of rotting meat for that, Wast.'

'Griffin, you've had your chance. I'll see you dead, the lot of you! Either that or work with me.'

'You?'

'Yeah. Hand Spiceland over as a rustler – your job as a lawman. I got proof he's been rustling. You're the sheriff – but I reckon you've got your loop tangled, Griffin. Side with me and you'll be safe – me and Judge Tarrant.'

'Huh! That goddam rogue! He's like you, Wast, a twister!'

Wast's scheme was pretty clear. He wanted to get rid of Ern so that the Round-O would be forced on to the market, for sale, by the County Administration when Ern failed to pay his mortgage dues. Wast would buy the place because no other rancher would want the almost grass-less land.

Jack Griffin felt an urge to shock Bertram Wast out of his confidence. 'How did you find out about the gold, Wast?' Jack's voice carried strongly right across the rock-girt valley.

'Gold?'

'You heard me, man! Yeah, gold. You knew it was somewhere on Ern Spiceland's arid land.'

Bertram Wast could not resist boasting. 'What you don't realise, Griffin, is that I worked on prospecting in my young days – before I made money in cattle and land deals – and I know signs of gold in the land. It's here, ain't it?' Wast's voice got excited. 'Damn you, Griffin, say I'm right! I know I'm right.'

'You're crazy! Only rock and rattlers up here, you fool.'

'You're trying to fool me!'

'You'll die an old man afore you find gold up here!' Jack took a delight in trying to shake Bertram Wast's confidence. He was damned if he'd give the villain a clue.

There was silence and then the rogue's voice snarled back over the land. 'All right, let's quit fooling! I got rid of Tom Mortimer and Sam Brant because they didn't work fast enough at getting Spiceland off his land. They took dinero from me but failed to deliver the goods and then they wanted to back out. I reckon Mortimer was going to blab – and Brant, too – but I never gave them the chance.'

Jack Griffin levelled his rifle around the boulder but he had no real target. The others in his party were waiting for action.

'I'm a-coming to get Spiceland!' shouted Bertram Wast. 'Me and my men will do your work, Griffin. He's a rustler – and folks around the ranches don't like dirty rustlers.'

'I reckon they don't like killers either!' Jack flung back across the silent rocky land.

It was rather obvious that Wast must know, if only by hunch, that the gold had been discovered. The truth was out on the side of both parties. But maybe the man did not realise they were hiding almost on top of the bonanza.

For some moments in the grim hiatus, Jack wondered why Wast had taken Otto Tribe into his confidence – and the other two hombres. Maybe Wast had bribed them with promises of big money or even hinted at the existence of gold. But surely the men would never live long enough to share gold with Bertram Wast? When their usefulness was over, they would be eliminated. Sure as heck, Wast would emerge as the only controller of the gold.

But that was speculation because right now Ern Spiceland was the owner of the land and he had friends and family. And Jack Griffin was after all the rightful sheriff of Greenlands and with some authority right beyond that area.

It seemed the edgy parley was over. A rifle barked from the opposite side of the narrow valley and the steel-jacketed slug bit into rocks close to Jack Griffin and Ern. Talk was seemingly over. Maybe Wast had given orders to fight.

If the hired men had the stomach for it, they would get some spitting slugs! Jack flattened on his stomach and poked his rifle around the boulder that sheltered him. He thought he saw a black patch against the lighter colour of the rising valley wall and he pressed his trigger twice. The dark patch seemed to disappear. The man had moved!

And then guns spoke from both sides of the valley as men fired in grim eagerness to blast someone out of this world. Death sprang from the greed for money! Jack fired back at a few dubious targets. Then he realised that this sort of battle could go on for a long time until one side was spent up with regard to ammunition.

Bullets whined into the boulders around them, spitting dust and chips of flying rock into the air. The horses in the rocky nook were spooked by the sudden gunfire but Jane was able to soothe them.

Bandy triggered into the fleeting targets on the other side of the rock-strewn valley and then started to curse and reload. 'Sure ain't nobody goin' to git killed over there! Them hombres are only stickin' their noses out! Can't hit a nose at this distance!'

Jack grinned and twisted around to see that Jane was all right. Anxious about the girl he sure admired, he realised she was only a school-teacher and no gun-handler! A shooting party was no place for her.

'Reckon you're right, Bandy,' he called out to the broad little man. 'Guess we could keep this up till nightfall.'

'I'd like to drill one of them bastards plumb dead!' yelled Bandy.

'I've got an idea,' said Jack suddenly.

Ern Spiceland looked at him interestedly. 'Yeah? Let's hear it.'

'Wal, we won't decide anythin' this way. We'll just use up all our shells and maybe have to ride out for safety when it's sundown. But we've got the dynamite.'

'Ah! Go on.'

'Two of us could climb a high rock overlooking them lot on tother side and sort o' look down on Wast's party.'

'Yeah?'

'Naturally Wast and his pals will see us moving an' maybe start throwing lead, but that's a chance we'll have to take. There are plenty of rocks to flop down behind. We take the dynamite with us. Got the idea?'

'You bet! Dynamite against guns.'

'Plenty of explosive power in dynamite. If we can climb to an overlookin' rock – one of them high pinnacles over there – we can lob explosive on to them galoots, murderous thugs every one of 'em!'

Bandy had heard the conversation. 'Hey! I want to be in on this lil stunt!'

'Why in tarnation?'

'Because iffen Mister Spiceland stops a slug there'll be no galoot around to protect the gal! That's why, darn it.'

'And what if you get lead poisoning?'

'Me? Hell, they cain't kill me! Now, lissen Mister Sheriff – I'll go with you. Anyways, I knows dynamite. Useter fool around with it when I worked at blastin' for the railroad.'

'You never told me that,' yelled Ern.

In the end Bandy Manners had his own way and he set off with Jack Griffin to work around to the nearest high pinnacle some way across the valley floor. Jack had opened a box of dynamite and they stuck the sticks in their belts and began to crawl over the intervening ground.

It was a hell of a chance he and Bandy were taking and he knew about it when Bertram Wast's thugs sighted their crawling figures and began to pump angry slugs at them. But the distance factor was in their favour. The slugs bit into ground all around them but were not too close for alarm. Still, an odd bullet might find them. Jack gritted his teeth and crawled on, yard after yard, dust in his mouth, the earth strangely warm. He and Bandy reached the base of the rocky pinnacle breathing relief. If an errant slug from the thugs on the other side had found the dynamite, the future would have been non-existent.

'Start climbing, Bandy.' Jack looked up at the rocky spire. If they reached the top they had a commanding position from which to throw down the dynamite sticks at their enemies.

As luck would have it, there were plenty of ledges and protrusions on the side of the strange old rocky pinnacle which helped them climb steadily to the top. But their progress had been sighted by Wast's hired gunnies and angry slugs whistled through the air. However, they reached the top of the spire of rock and snuggled into concealment among the clefts. Then they had time to assess the positions of the gang below.

It seemed that Wast's gunnies simply thought the two men were only seeking a better position from which to shoot their irons. They did not know about the dynamite concealed in their belts and, of course, from the distance, they could not see the green sticks.

Jack could see Ern and Fred down below, another advantage if and when they got around to lobbing dynamite because they did not want to blow up their own kind.

'That greedy swine has no idea about the explosives,' Jack snapped over to Bandy.

'Yeah. Sure figures we're here to shoot better,' agreed Bandy. 'Wal, we'll teach him a trick or two.'

'Any good at lobbing dynamite, old-timer?' asked Jack.

'Good at lighting the fuses, too,' returned the other man. 'I told you, I useter do blasting when we was cutting through rock for the railroad.'

'That's a useful skill,' said Jack Griffin. 'Wal, are we

goin' to start raising hell down there among Wast's hellions?'

'I'm ready, Mister Sheriff. Is this kinda lawful, huh?'

Jack stared back grimly at the man. 'If we stay down there in the valley, Wast and his hired gun-hands will pin us down for such a long time we'll run out of ammunition.'

Jack brought out the sticks of dynamite and a box of long-stemmed sulphur matches. At that moment, he felt bitterly ruthless. Wast had forced him into this situation. The man had threatened death long enough to those who stood in his way. Knowing about the gold now as he did, he'd probably be able to buy sufficient lawless men to smash Ern and himself at will, given the chance.

Bertram Wast wouldn't get that chance!

'We'll light the fuses, Bandy,' snapped Jack Griffin bitterly.

8
Place of Death

Bandy Manners had no scruples. 'You durned bet I'll light the fuses, Mister Griffin!'

It was the work of a few minutes to get some fuses lighted with the sulphur matches, while they hid down among the clefts in the rock. The two men watched them burn a little so that they would be near to detonation when they hit the ground below.

Jack flung the first one over and Bandy followed suit, taking great care with the killer stuff and trying not to get in each other's way. Swiftly, they lighted two more and lobbed them over at their specific targets down below in the valley, where they could see Wast and his hired thugs. Jack realised that a throw wasn't as accurate as an aimed gun but the dynamite had power to spread.

They were busy lighting the remaining sticks when the roar of the first explosion hit their ears. They could not see much, as they crouched in hiding, but the noise was frightening. Jack knew the grim inner feeling when he thought of other men dying violently. He supposed it had to be this way. With Fred and Jane in their party below in the valley, they could not take risks. Wast would kill them if he thought they were witnesses to any killing his men might undertake. And as for self-defence, only Ern could shoot with any accuracy. Fred was not the gun-toting kind.

When the noise had faded away, echoes of the blasts dying out, Jack took a look at the scene down below his rocky pinnacle. He hoped Fred, Jane and Ern were all right. They were well away from where the blast had happened, a good way opposite from Wast and his killer types.

The rocky-strewn ground below seemed pretty much the same, the same pattern, but there was evidence where soil and rock had been violently disturbed. He saw the shattered body of a horse, blood and flesh unpleasantly red. He swung his glance to the other side of the valley, hoping to see sign of Jane, her brother and Ern but there was nothing moving. He was sure they were hiding, way off from where the explosion had taken place.

Bandy was staring down, too. 'Did we git them hellions?'

As if it was some sort of anwer, Jack Griffin was suddenly amazed to see two riders cruelly rowelling their horses down the valley, seemingly wanting to escape a situation they did not like.

Jack stared in disbelief. One rider was Bertram Wast, his black clothes unmistakeable, and the other was the gunny Otto Tribe. They were urging their mounts to frantic limits, hoofs stabbing at the uneven earth and the nostrils of the horses snorting in fear.

Ern and Fred were out in the open, firing at the fleeing targets, but the jerking animals were not easy to hit and, of course, Fred was no gun-hand. And in actual fact both men were using hand-guns for some erratic reason. With every passing second the fleeing horsemen got further out of range.

'Can you believe that?' snarled Bandy.

'That hombre – Wast – must have a charmed life!'

'D'you reckon we got the other two rannies?'

'Seems like it. Wast and Tribe must have been quick to grab a cayuse the moment they saw the dynamite come down and before it exploded on the ground. Seconds in all, I guess.'

'Dynamite plays strange tricks, Mister Griffin. Maybe those two were behind some rocky cover when the stuff exploded.'

'There's some explanation like that, Bandy.'

'When men get buffeted by explosive they are usually dazed and helpless.'

'Not those two, Bandy. Hell, they are gettin' right away down the blasted valley in spite of Ern and Fred taking potshots at them.'

'An' we're stuck up here on a rock!' snarled Bandy Manners.

'Wal, let's get down, old man. Sure as hell we ain't goin' to catch Bertram Wast.'

'Beats me how baddies allus get the edge,' Bandy growled and began to grab at hand-holds for the descent of the rocky spire of rock that had been their vantage-point. Jack Griffin followed the oldser but at a slightly faster rate of progress, finally reaching the base, and then he ran for the other side of the valley, towards Jane, Ern and Fred Spiceland. Rifles impeded their run: Colts were firmly wedged in holsters and the dynamite had been used. As Bandy and Jack ran, they saw the spot which had hidden Wast and his ruffian hands. They saw two dead horses and two spreadeagled men, in a mutilated condition, red flesh a gory sight.

Two more of Wast's hired hands had paid the price.

Jack Griffin reached Jane as she came forward to meet him and it seemed natural to take her into his arms, a sweet experience for a man sometimes shy with women.

'You are not hurt?' She searched his face.

'And you're fine, Jane? Thank God!'

'You saw Was and his sidekick get away?' This from Ern. 'We sure tried to take him with our handguns. Should have used the rifles but in the commotion we left 'em on the ground.'

'Dead men!' whispered Jane. 'I hate this violence, Jack.'

'I know you do. But don't waste any sympathy on them. Those trigger-happy swines were only happy when gunning for someone else.'

'Them jiggers are buzzard bait now,' yelled Bandy, delighted. 'But buzzards is bad luck. You don't want 'em in this valley of yourn, Mister Spiceland, not with the gold around hyar. So we should get 'em buried mighty fast!'

'In that case, Bandy, you got a job,' said Jack gravely. 'I remember we packed some shovels. Figure you could do the burying?'

'Hell!' There was chagrin on the oldster's face but he went off for a shovel. Ern and Jack grinned at the old fellow. And then Ern turned seriously to the sheriff. 'Maybe this gun-play will make Wast stick to his Bar-K land!'

'I doubt that. Bertram Wast will know by now by instinct that you've located the gold somewhere around here, although not the exact spot. That greedy son-of-a-bitch ain't easily put off.'

'I aim to beat him, then. Or any other rough-neck that aims to come snooping around this valley. The land is mine by right of legal deed. I think I'll build a wire fence right across this valley.'

'It's your land.'

'Yeah, but don't forget we all share in this gold bonanza. You have fought with me against Wast.' Ern grinned at Bandy. 'And you, too, old-timer. You're in on any gold we dig out or pick up.'

'Heh! Heh! Reckon I'll be rich!'

'Don't drink it all away.'

'Do you think that putting up a wire fence will keep strangers out?' inquired Fred Spiceland.

Ern looked thoughtful. 'Maybe not.'

'Reckon it will attract nosy rannies,' said Jack. 'And Wast will be among the first of them.'

'Let's have a long talk,' muttered Ern. He waved to the others, including Bandy. Then he turned to Jack. 'You say it all. You know what's in my mind.'

When they were ready, Jack Griffin began to outline things. 'It's thisaway. Ern reckons we're all partners in this gold claim but personally I don't want to feel I'm grabbin'. Anyway, Ern figures it would be a good idea to fence the valley off to keep out strangers. But I say this: we'll try to keep this find secret. We can keep this secret for a while, maybe. Wast and his sidekick have a hunch the gold is here — they're bound to think that — but I'm pretty sure they won't go around telling all and sundry in Greenlands that there is gold in this lonely, rocky valley. And we won't either. We won't say a word for as long as possible. I reckon the truth will emerge when we begin to lodge the gold with the assayer's office in Abilene. The news will sure get around. But that gives Ern time to organise everything in this valley.'

'So we keep the news of the gold find to ourselves,' muttered Ern Spiceland.

'More than that. I vote we keep all the gold we

retrieve from that rocky cleft in the valley floor – the easy pickings in the shape of the nuggets – until we take it in bulk to the assayer. That'll give us time to maybe build a shanty up here, apart from the tents, and the wire fence.'

'I reckon you'll need a wire fence horse-high, hog-tight and bull-strong,' yelled Bandy.

'Won't some galoot come along and wonder what's going on?' asked Fred.

'Not many wanderers come out here,' said Ern. 'An' if some nosy ranny does come, we'll say we're borin' for water.'

'That'll shut up some but not Bertram Wast.' Jack Griffin stared around, at the sun, now at its midday height and knew the daylight would recede from this moment. 'Wal, we'll mine as much gold as possible in the shape of easily-handled nuggets from that cleft before we take the trail to the assayer in Abilene. And we button up our lips. Maybe there'll be trouble from Wast. I sure don't know. But that lousy villain can't chase you off your land now that you know the secret. He can't break you now that you've got gold.'

'He could come shootin',' yelled Bandy.

'And he's still got the cows with the worked-over brands,' Jane reminded them.

'We'll handle that problem when it comes,' said Jack Griffin. 'And I reckon I've got to get back to town. I'm the sheriff there an' folks might want to know what the hell I'm doin' away from the office. Sure would like to give you a hand in rakin' up them gold nuggets.'

Ern slapped his back. 'You've done more than your share when you and Bandy fixed those damned villains with the dynamite. Get back to town, Jack, and deal with Wast if he figures to make grief for me with those beeves he planted on my range. And you can take Jane back to that hotel.'

'But I want to help,' protested the girl. 'I've only another two days and then I've got to go back to my teaching in Abilene.'

'This ain't the place for a gal. So git!'

'Oh, you!'

Ern Spiceland's decision was right because there could be no guarantee that Bertram Wast might not return in an effort to kill them, get rid of them and search for sign of the gold himself. Gold stirred evil men to desperate deeds. Wast, who had wealth enough, coveted more wealth. This was the nature of totally evil greedy men. They just wanted more. Gold surpassed anything that land and cattle could provide. Wast wanted more and more power.

Jack got to the saddle of his roan as Jane Spiceland climbed to her mount. Although she was disappointed, she realised it was not actually possible for her to stay out in this rough place, with possible danger from gunhands. Of course, she wanted to help her brothers. They had work to do, setting up the camp, getting the wire out for the fence, seeing to the horses and numerous jobs that would keep them busy till sundown.

They eventually rode out of the gold valley, waving good-bye for the moment. He liked the lithe figure she made as she sat the saddle, so boyish and yet essentially feminine. When all this gun-play and grief was over he'd have to tell Jane how he felt about her!

They cantered the horses as soon as they found fairly flat land away from the broken country and made some speed. They found a trail that led by the Round-O ranch and eventually to Greenlands. They found, too, that there was plenty to talk about. They discussed the gold, Bertram Wast and his now readily apparent villainies, and the future, especially the future. The gold had altered everything, although this sudden wealth had not yet sunk into their minds. Ezra Hide, the old gold-hound, had altered their lives. Ern had now no pressing need to make money by ranching. Jane could leave teaching, if she so wanted. And the job of sheriff, while affording satisfaction, was not everything if gold was bringing wealth to them all!

They were riding out in a wide loop, a few miles west of the Round-O spread, on the way to the town of Greenlands, when Jack spied a cloud of dust.

He surmised it was caused by a small herd of cattle on the move. They were being driven hard, prodded on by men and not merely wandering. They were not spooked but being kept in a controlled bunch by trail hands, he guessed, and so close to the Round-O, Ern's land. He guessed they were leery Texas longhorns but he and Jane were not close enough to identify the trail waddies.

He had a sudden good hunch that these men were Wast's hired hands from the Bar-K range and they were rounding up the cattle with the altered brands. Ern and Bandy certainly were not working cattle, being miles away in the gold valley!

'Guess it's Wast again – or his men,' Jack spoke to the girl. 'Now why is he driving those beeves to Greenlands?'

The girl shook her head and kept on riding close to Jack Griffin. He, for his part, decided that there was nothing to be gained by getting close to the herd or the range hands. In fact, he wanted to see Jane back to the safety of the Packhorse Hotel in town. And as for the cattle, altered brands or not, Wast could have them! Their value was low compared to the wealth in the gold valley on Ern's land.

The longish ride came to an end when the sun finally moved redly to the horizon. A little weary after the rough trail ride, Jane went to her hotel, anticipating a bath, nice food and a good bed. Jack Griffin allowed his horse to plod on to the sheriff's office and to the livery at the rear. Then, back at his quarters, he pondered the events of the long day. It was hard to believe, so far away from the valley in the broken country, that he could be a rich man, along with Ern, Jane, Fred and Bandy! All they had to do was get the gold nuggets safely collected from that strange cleft in the rocky land, and, in fact, proceed to mine the gold-bearing quartz.

He shook his head sadly as he thought of poor old Ezra, so close to his dream of a bonanza but now dead, struck down by the likes of Wast and his gunmen.

A bit later he stripped and washed the sweat and dust from his body and felt better in a new red and black check shirt. He got out a new pair of pants from his belongings in the quarters. They were brown and tan and in the fashion of the day. He got into some new riding boots and gave them a lick with a polishing rag. Then he pinned his sheriff's badge to the clean shirt and felt more like a new man. He strapped on his gun-belt again, checked the Colt and then decided he was ready to eat. His hat was dusty but he beat out the trail stuff with some vigorous shakes and then went out.

His first stop was China Joe's eating-house where the smell of real food made him realise he was almost starving. He ordered steak and coffee, a huge mug, steaming hot. He grinned at the Chinese waiter. 'Hi, Johnnie! Make that steak real big, huh!'

'Sure thing, Sir!' The little Chink knew him and smiled widely.

It was some time later when he came out of China Joe's place, the sun now vanished from the day and lanterns of kerosene lighted in Greenland's main drag. Jack Griffin felt tired. Maybe he had eaten too much! Maybe it was time to hit the hay!

That all changed when he saw Otto Tribe walk stiffly into the Red Pine saloon and disappear into the smoke-filled noisy dive.

Grimly, he knew he still had work to do!

Summarising things in his mind, he knew with Ern Spiceland he had found the answers to many questions about Bertram Wast and his motives, but men had been killed in the doing, good men, friends. It was not just enough to know that they had beaten Wast to the discovery of the gold. The murders of Tom Mortimer, Sam Brant and Ezra must be avenged, hopefully with justice.

He had retaliated. He had eliminated Red Holbin and Jed Slacks, not to mention the crazy Mexican Wast had hired. And he had captured Mike Capstaff, only to have the man killed unlawfully by the lethal Wast or his men.

He could not hang up his guns or quit the sheriff's office until he had brought Wast to book and any of his men – and that must include Otto Tribe.

The man had ordered a drink and was standing alone and looking morosely around the bar. As his natural expression was sufficiently ugly, that was no addition to his good looks!

Jack moved quietly to the counter and jerked a glance to the bartender. The man slid the whiskey along and slowly wiped his hands on a cloth.

Jack Griffin quietly turned and faced Otto Tribe,

leaning with his right arm on the counter. He could see the long scar on the man's dark lean face.

'You can tell Wast that I'm still comin' after him.' Sure, it was a taunt. Jack just watched the guy.

Otto Tribe faced the sheriff in the same manner, his movements slow, deliberate, eyes fixed grimly on the lawman.

'You're welcome to ride out to the spread any time, hombre.'

'Figure to be waitin' for me, huh?'

'Yeah. Could be. Wast ain't finished – an' neither am I. We sure don't like bastards who play with dynamite.'

'Dynamite is sure hard to handle.'

'You son-of-a-bitch! Sheriff, shit! Dynamite is for a hellion who ain't so good with a gun!'

Jack smiled and watched the man narrowly. 'You didn't like it!'

'Bastard badge-toter!'

'You want to reach for your hog-leg?'

'Some day, pig-man!'

'Quit callin' me names an' go for your iron.'

'Some day! Damn you!'

The man wasn't to be prodded into gun action. Jack tried another tactic. 'I want the names of the waddies who did the branding job.'

'What brandin' job?'

'The worked-over brands on the beef you were driving out of the Round-O range just a few hours ago.'

Otto Tribe jeered. 'Got your rope in a twist, sheriff shit! I wasn't on that job. Other men, sure thing, on the boss's payroll. Wast has plenty of hands.'

'Keep talkin'.'

'Hell, you figure you can do anything? Wast will

have you kilt some day. He's got a nice play figured with them beeves. He's bringin' them into town. Gonna put them in the cattle corrals. Figures to show the folks of this town that Spiceland is a goddam rustler an' you know that ain't popular in a cattle town. Then maybe he can git a posse o' men who think like him and take the law into his own hands. And if some git shot deader than carrion, then it'll be too bad!'

'Quite a speech! Thanks for the information.'

'Drop dead! Go screw that Spiceland dame! You're a dead guy, sheriff!'

Jack tossed his glass of whiskey into the leering face, angry as all hell at the scathing, dirty remarks. For some seconds the man blinked and rubbed at his eyes.

Jack Griffin brought his fist back angrily and then smashed it into the ramrod's jaw. The heavy man staggered back under the one solid, vengeful punch. He rammed into a table nearby, cracking the wood leg under the impact.

Seething at the ugly man's sneering remarks, Jack followed up and crashed two more bunched fists into the swarthy face as the ramrod of the Bar-K lurched away and tried to draw a gun from leather. Jack got a grip on the man's wrist and as the gun eased out he jerked savagely. The big Colt .45 clattered to the floor. Well, at least the hellion had tried to draw!

The other men in the saloon sidled to the walls in order to give the combatants more room, watching warily for gun-play. No man wanted to get in the way of a stray slug!

A fist cracked on bone, Jack's cheek-bone! The sheriff staggered back, realising that this hell-bent had plenty of steam left to throw into a punch. His back to the pine bar-top, Jack used it as a spring-board and propelled himself at the big ruffian. He crashed into the ramrod and they both lurched into a wood partition and the structure shuddered under the weight and splintered.

Jack Griffin tried another tactic, swinging a slow heavy blow into the man's guts and the guy grimaced in agony. Jack deliberately rammed another fist into the soft belly, wanting to hurt this hellion gun-hand, Wast's segundo. The man gave a sickening groan, like a low-class creature under sentence of death. But fist-fighting would not kill this man. Jack Griffin pitched another ramming blow near to the man's heart. Maybe the dirt would have a heart attack which would save the price of a slug or the hangman's rope!

It was the only way to deal with a vicious gun-thug. As the man staggered back again, Jack crashed his weight against Otto Tribe and kept the man's arms pinned. Then he chopped grimly at the bloodied ugly face. Otto Tribe staggered as if drunk.

'I want to know who did the branding job! Who made the iron?'

Still the man did not answer. In fact, he tried to lurch out of the sheriff's reach. So Jack slammed further savage punishment into the contorted face and the man began to blab.

'I made the iron! Me an' Eli White roped an' branded them beeves! We drove 'em to Round-O range! Ahhh! Cut it out, damn yuh! Ahhh!'

'Wal, I got a cell for you!' panted Jack Griffin. 'Maybe you can confess a bit more when you got time to figure it out!'

He hustled the man to the batwing doors and then stopped, Otto Tribe dribbling blood and groaning.

'Did you fellers hear that confession?' Jack asked the

watching bar customers.

There was silence while the drinkers looked dubiously at each other. 'Don't rightly get what it's all about,' said one.

'All right. I'm arrestin' this galoot for the murder of a prospector by the name of Ezra Hide.'

'Did he kill that old buzzard?' asked a puncher.

'I figure to prove it soon.'

But the parley had given Otto Tribe time to clear his head and summon up new strength. With a sudden leap he was free from Jack's hands. He crashed through the batwing doors and ran over the boardwalk, scattering two men in the street. He leaped with new speed to his horse, At that moment tied to the hitching-rail. He was on the animal, fast as a fugitive animal, by the time Jack got to the boardwalk.

Jack was on the dusty street, gun in hand, hesitating for vital seconds when Otto Tribe jabbed cruel spurs to his animal and wheeled it in more seconds. The horse jumped forward in fright. Before Jack Griffin could leap clear the horse had knocked him down.

As Jack sprawled, the animal cleared him by sheer instinct. Jack lay on the dusty ground, dazed, time not on his side. Then Otto Tribe brought his horse back, a dirty trick in the man's evil mind. He reared the animal above Jack's head, tugging at the leathers to get the creature's hoofs high above the sheriff's head as he sprawled. The animal's iron-clad hoofs stabbed air high above Jack Griffin's head.

Then Otto Tribe brought the plunging foreleg down with all the horse's weight behind them, right at the sheriff's head!

9
Wast's Last Move

It was just by a desperate twist that Jack rolled over in the dust like a curled ball, clearing the plunging hoofs as they kicked heavily into the road, raising dust and chips of gravel. Griffin slithered away and the Bar-K ramrod urged the horse forward and once again reared the hoofs high.

There was not time for the sheriff of Greenlands to get to his feet. A horrible death stared at him. Jack's only movement were a desperate rolling and scrambling as the horse's forelegs slashed down again at his head. But by a miracle the hoofs of the frightened animal missed him by inches. Otto Tribe was trying to kill him!

For the third time Jack Griffin rolled clear of the plunging horse, and then, seeing there was a split second of time given to him, he leaped to his feet.

In one fast movement, he crouched, heart thumping in fear – yes, fear – and his gun was in his hand.

Otto Tribe wheeled his big heavy horse again, jabbing rowels wickedly into the animal's flesh, and urged the mount towards the sheriff. The ramrod's face was twisted with hate.

In the seconds given to him, Jack had no option but to use the trigger. The Colt spat flame in the evening light from the nearby street lanterns. And then a second spurt of flame, in seconds. The explosions crashed across the street.

Otto Tribe pitched from the saddle and hit the ground as if a giant fist had thrown him from the saddle leather. The horse slithered to its haunches in fright and veered away. Jack Griffin jumped back, stumbling in his haste.

The gunfire brought men to the scene, from the saloon, punchers, other men, staring. As if by magic old Doc Turner was there, from heaven knows where! 'Another dead 'un! Goshdarn it, this town will be in debt this year owin' to burial parties!'

Jack stuck his hardware back in the holster, wiping the sweat from his brow with his green bandanna. He stared morosely at the dead man, fancying he could smell the odour of blood. Suddenly, he felt a hatred of his gun and of the men who were forcing this kind of play on him.

But the man had tried to ride him down and kill him. He could have been smashed to red pulp by plunging hoofs.

He walked slowly away in the direction of the livery. Although tired to the bone, he felt impelled to go on. Fifteen minutes later he rode a fresh horse out of Greenlands.

He wished he could stop and say good-night to Jane Spiceland but if he told her he was riding out to the Bar-K ranch and that area she would try to deter him.

It was really dark but with a moon riding into the night sky and there'd be light aplenty for the trail out. His Colt was full of shells and the rifle in the saddle-holster was checked.

Almost at once, just clear of the town, he rode into the small herd of cattle. He recognised the longhorns as the over-branded beef that had been planted on Ern's range, a whole darned herd of them! In addition, he recognised Bertram Wast astride his big horse. With him, prodding the cattle, were two other punchers. Jack did not know these hands.

Jack Griffin pulled his horse into the shelter of a few cottonwoods that lined this part of the trail to Greenlands. He acted swiftly before the other men had time to see him. A shadow in the moonlight, they had not sighted him. He waited among the cottonwoods and the cattle came on. They were lean Texas longhorns, leery at being driven at night. Wast came on, riding point, away from his men.

As the greedy murderous man rode past the cottonwood clump, Jack edged his horse out of the gloom. He had a rifle at the ready, a lethal repeating Remington, fast as a fury.

'Keep your hands high, Wast!'

The man turned his head, froze indecisively for a second and then slowly held his hands up at shoulder level. All at once a cloud scudded past the moon and light showed on Wast's hawk-like face. He even smiled. 'You!'

'Me, you swine!'

The two waddies on the other side of the herd halted their horses and stared at the intruder. 'Don't move to your guns,' Jack advised. 'That's right. Act sensible. I'm the sheriff of Greenlands.'

Wast was still-incredibly-smiling. 'You can't get away with this fool play, Griffin.'

'Where are you going with these longhorns?'

'Taking them into town. Kinda evidence of rustling. My hands can testify they were found on Round-O range.'

Jack let him have it. 'Otto Tribe is dead.'

Bertram Wast lost his smile momentarily. 'Is that so? Who murdered him? You? Guess the folks of this town should string you up!'

'You're the hombre who'll get strung up. You've over-played your hand tryin' to get more wealth. All this about rustling cows! It's played out, Wast, you damned fool. You can't get Ern Spiceland off his land.'

A struggle was going on within Bertram Wast, the outward signs the flicker in his eyes, uncertain for once in his hard life. His mouth twisted. He was thinking he was beaten. This sheriff had the drop on him.

'You can't pin anything on me, Griffin. Have you got proof of your cockeyed stories? You'll have to take me before a judge in Abilene and that judge is a friend of mine.'

Jack breathed hard. He knew Wast played a good hand. Jack jerked his rifle as a hint. 'Right now you can take these beeves back to your ranch and I'm a-goin' with you.'

With his rifle as a persuading force, he rode around the herd and made the men turn the herd. Jack kept the riders before him all the time, his eyes on Wast principally. When the herd was turned back from the trail to town, he rode up close behind Bertram Wast. All at once Jack heard one puncher say to another. 'I'll ride drag, Eli.'

Jack smiled. He wanted to talk to this man called Eli White, for Eli White was the hand who had helped Otto Tribe alter the brands on the cows.'

Jack did not get much chance to speak to the hand until they had the herd back on Bar-K range and they were near the ranch buildings. The man was a scraggy rannigan with bright gimlet eyes as if he was continually scheming.

Bertram Wast rode calmly, making no attempt at trickery. Jack wondered if the rancher packed a gun. There was no sign of a weapon, no holster. But Wast had no compunction about murder, although it seemed his method was to pay other men to kill.

Suddenly Jack called a halt to the drive. The Bar-K buildings were just ahead, screened by cottonwoods. 'All right, Eli White, you can ride with me.' Jack paused. 'Wast and his hands can push this beef right to the fences of the Bar-K ranch.'

'What d'you want with me, Sheriff?'

'I want you to sign a statement right back in my office.'

'I ain't signin' nothing!' And Eli White looked uncertainly at his boss, Bertram Wast, as everything halted.

'But I figure you will, Eli. I want a statement from you saying you helped Otto Tribe to alter the brands of some cattle from Bar-K to Round-O and then drove the critturs on to Ern Spiceland's spread. This statement will say that the scheme was part of a plan to frame Ern Spiceland for rustling an' that the hombre who figured it out was Mister Bertram Wast.'

Eli White laughed uncertainly. 'You must think I'm crazy. Sure, I'll come with you as long as you point that rifle at me but I ain't signin' nothing!'

With triumph in his sneering voice, the man glanced again at Bertram Wast and they both smiled.

'You'll come with me,' said Jack Griffin. 'And I'll tell you why.' He paused. The wan moonlight played on the strange scene, the riders and their mounts and the straggle of cattle.

'Spit it out, Lawman.'

'You'll come with me into town and sign because your life isn't worth a Mex dollar. You're dangerous to your boss because you know too much. I reckon you know more about Wast than just the brandin' job. I figure you were one of the riders who tried to burn the Round-O ranch-house. An' maybe you were one of the rannigans who made off with Jed Slack's body. Your testimony could fix Wast good an' proper.'

There was only a snarling sound from Eli White.

'I know you wouldn't cross Wast in the ordinary way,' snapped the sheriff. 'No reward – an' plenty of risk. Wast knew that when he hired you. But I've got plenty of money to tempt you, Eli.'

'What the hell!'

'Testify against Bertram Wast and you can have as much as you want.' Jack reflected on the gold lying up there in the gold valley. 'Remember, your life ain't worth much to Wast. He'll have you turned into cadaver meat just as soon as look at you. It will pay you to ride back with me. I got dinero in the bank for spot payment, feller.'

Jack watched the man carefully and saw his gimlet eyes look at Wast uneasily.

'He's bluffing you, Eli,' said Bertram Wast.

The man snarled. 'Yeah? Like hell he is! Maybe he's right.'

'You're a fool, Eli!' Wast suddenly shouted.

'Two thousand dollars for you right now if you can give me evidence. For good evidence, the right sort, two thousand dollars and the chance to hit the border. Plenty of places in Mexico where a hombre with that kind of loot can fix himself up mighty fine. Drink an' women a-plenty, huh! Stick with Wast an' you'll die of a slug in the gut. You're too dangerous to let live, Eli.'

The man glowered at Bertram Wast for some moments. The seeds of doubt were there.

'This man is bluffing,' snapped Wast. 'You can't prove anything against me, not a runt like you.'

'Runt, huh! Yeah? I kin talk plenty – iffen I want to an' for two thousand dollars.'

'He hasn't got that kind of money.'

'Oh, but I have.' Jack nodded at Eli White. 'It's yours an' a horse to the border damn fast if you sign a statement.'

'Don't let him outsmart you, Eli.' Wast was angry.

'He ain't. An' you ain't neither, Mister Wast. I was in that firin' party when we tried to burn the Round-O buildings. An' I was one o' the hands who got Jed Slacks out o' the sheriff's office. I kin talk plenty – an' I can write my name.' The puncher's voice rose to a shrill note. 'This jigger is right – an' he's the sheriff. You're trying to get rid of me. Red Holbin's gone – so's Otto Tribe, I hear – an' those fellers up in the broken country.'

'That's mighty fine reasoning,' said Jack. 'And true. You comin' along with me, hombre? I'm gettin' mighty sick of holding this Remington.'

'Sure, I'm a-comin'!' The man wheeled his horse.

'I'll dispute that man's word,' snarled Wast.

As Eli White turned from his boss, Bertram Wast rode away with his other hands and the remainder of the herd. It seemed the argument was over for the night.

Jack Griffin returned to Greenlands and stuck Eli White in a cell. The man protested. 'What about that money?'

'You'll get it tomorrow, you snivelling rat, as promised, an' you'll hit for the border tomorrow – if an' when that statement is fine and signed.'

Grimly, he sent a passer-by for Doc Turner, Joe Blade and the manager of the Packhorse Hotel. He knew they would grumble at the late hour but they were all reputable men in the town and would make good winesses.

When they arrived, Jack said: 'As sheriff I'm askin' you men to stick around for some time as witnesses to anything that might happen. And then maybe later you can sign as witnesses to a written statement.'

Puzzled, they nodded and grumbled. Then the sheriff asked them to hide in a large storeroom at the rear of the sheriff's office. 'If I'm wrong, gents, I'll apologise, but I've got a hunch we'll get a visitor. A certain lousy skunk may think I'm in the Packhorse with you fellers.'

If he was right, he thought he would not have long to wait.

For fully twenty minutes Jack and the other men waited in the dark room, full of tense, grim curiosity. Then a key scraped in the front door at the other end of the passage. A man with a key! He was a man who had no right to a key to the sheriff's office!

Then the man walked quietly and confidently along the passage towards the position of the cells. Jack nodded tersely at the men with him in the storeroom.

He knew the intruder was Bertram Wast! He knew this because he expected the visit!

Wast was in the office, near the cell which housed Eli White! Jack Griffin moved partly out of the storeroom, softly, like an Indian on the prowl. His hand was close to his Colt. A man's voice cursed and screamed. 'No! You skunk! Don't shoot, Wast! I won't talk!'

Eli White was shouting for his life. At that moment

Jack Griffin stepped clear into the room fronting the cells.

'Wast!' he called softly.

The big man in the black suit turned with surprising lithe speed. There was a little Derringer in the hand of the man who usually did not pack a gun! In the semi-darkness the dull-plated little gun barked and Jack Griffin felt a red-hot pain stab his chest.

Jack squeezed the trigger of his own gun as the pain hurt like hell. As the little Derringer spat a slug again, a Colt slug from the sheriff's gun tore into Wast's heart. Jack put out a hand to steady himself against the wall. He swayed. Then he saw the unbelievable.

Bertram Wast was still standing on his feet, a contorted look on his face which seemed like a grin. But it was sheer pain. A patch of red blood welled around his black jacket.

And then, with a horrible gasp, the rancher slowly slid sideways and buckled to the office floor.

As the other men crowded into the room, Jack gasped: 'I figured he'd – try – to kill Eli White. I couldn't git him any other way. Gunsmoke sure took charge of the – other – hombres – who might have given – evidence –'

And then Jack Griffin passed out and went into a pit of darkness!

A few days later he was in bed, sitting up and looking pretty cheerful because Jane was there and Doc Turner.

'Guess you'll patch up,' cackled the medical man. 'A Derringer bullet ain't nothing. Wast is sure dead. That feller, Eli White, spilled the beans, but good.'

'Are you going to give him his money?' asked Jane.

'Yeah, give the rat his dinero. It won't do him much good I reckon. But it's over, ain't it?'

Doc Turner waved and ambled out of the bedroom. Jack stared appreciatively at the girl, as well he might because she was lovely in her best gingham dress.

'You look mighty pretty!'

'Do you like me? I mean – really like me?'

'Jane – I love you,' he said boldly, amazed at himself.

She suddenly placed her lips to his and he held her tightly. 'I want to marry you, Jane.'

'Oh, Jack, just get better – quickly. I'll marry you whenever you want and I don't care if it's cattle or gold as long as I'm your wife!'

'That's why I'm hangin' up my guns. This town can get a new sheriff!'

'Oh, Jack, if I'm your wife I don't mind what work you choose to do!'